Ghost Owl

Nancy Schoellkopf

Cover design by Karen Phillips
Cover photo credits:
Young woman at night by Javier Allegue Barros on Unsplash
Owl by Ian Sherriffs on Shutterstock
Author by Leslie Rose, cropping by John Crandall

GHOST OWL

Nancy Schoellkopf

For the Thursday Night Writing Group

My Home Base

Chapter One
Mariah's Journal

I am dreaming but I don't know it yet. I am hovering somewhere high and misty, watching myself walk down a long narrow hallway. I look small and discouraged, as insubstantial as a pale sheet of paper. My auburn hair looks oily and limp; my shoulders are slumped. My brown eyes shine amber like a cat's.

Suddenly I am staring at my hands, as if a camera has just zoomed in for a close-up. Balanced on my palms I hold a small porcelain plate, and on the plate is a slice of cinnamon toast.

I love cinnamon toast, so fragrant and buttery, evocative of childhood late night snacks, the gritty texture of sugar against my molars.

The plate, the toast, my own hands become large and intensely vivid. I embody the dream, and the dream is sadness, because this one little piece of cinnamon toast will never be enough.

Most nights when I had the dream I carried long cookie sheets filled with brownies or lemon bars. In one dream I held a platter of sauerbraten and potato dumplings drenched in sweet ginger gravy. That night I awoke flooded with a bittersweet nostalgic ache, remembering the many hours I'd spent as a child watching my father cook. Sauerbraten was a rare winter treat, adapted from a recipe handed down from his German grandmother. More often he experimented with potatoes and cheese, fish and coconut milk, generous splashes of juice from freshly squeezed lemons and limes.

I often sat at the kitchen table, sketching crayoned drawings of the still life arrangements he had inadvertently assembled on the counter: sprigs of mint, bottles of Paul Newman's salad dressing and bumpy bits of ginger root. As I grew older I would take notes, hoping I might hit pay dirt and capture a recipe or two that would be worth repeating myself someday, for my father's dishes were always one of a kind, appearing tonight on this dining room table to make a debut and a finale at one and the same time, a creation so spontaneous that it couldn't be re-created if he tried. In some ways this delighted my father, reflecting as it did the precious and temporal nature of life itself. My mother seemed resigned to this quirky stubbornness her husband espoused, his refusal to write down a guide for next time. "He cooks the way he lives, Mariah," she used to tell me. "He follows the energy and there's nothing I can do to change him. I stopped trying to tame him long ago."

He follows the energy. That sentiment is worth noting now, though I didn't think much of it at the time.

When I told my mother about the sauerbraten dream she reached across the table to take my hand. "I miss Daddy too," she said, and even now—two and a half years after his death—I could hear her voice catch.

I squeezed my mother's hand and cleared my throat. "I don't think the dream is really about Daddy," I told her. Her eyes narrowed as I told her about the children. For that is how the dream always ends. I open the door at the end of the corridor, and I am confronted by dozens and dozens of hungry children.

When I first started having the dream they looked like thin but greedy American children in khakis and T shirts, rushing forward to grab whatever food I was offering. What followed was always a rumble of caustic words and frantic shouts as they elbowed and punched at me and one another, each struggling for a tiny handful of nourishment.

Now most often the children look like the starving third world babies I've seen on the news: their bellies distended, their limbs brittle and stick-thin. They are too weak to approach me. I stand in the doorway with my small offering, knowing that I cannot save even one of these children with cookies or potato dumplings.

My mother looked shaken, her hand pressed above her breasts. "When I was very young," she confided, "I used to dream that I was trying to count to infinity. I'd wake up in a panic, hot and agitated."

Now I knew she understood. "That's exactly how I feel!" I said.

She called my godfather, and had me tell him my dream on the phone. My godfather's name is Craig, and he used to work with my mother, even before she knew my father. She met Craig her first year of teaching, when the kids, the parents and the principal were so tough, she was beginning to wonder if she was going to last long term in this profession. Craig was the spiritual master playing the role of night custodian who came in one day and pulled her through.

"It sounds like a fear-based dream," he said simply.

"No," I insisted, "I don't feel afraid. I feel overwhelmed! I feel--" I paused, embarrassed. "I feel ashamed," I confessed. "I feel so ashamed and inadequate."

He was silent for a long time. "Craig?" I said tentatively,

suspecting the connection had been lost.

"This is a very important dream," he said suddenly. "This dream has a message for you. Before you go to sleep, you must ask the dream to speak to you in a more direct way. To let you in on its secret."

I was disappointed and a little annoyed. "Can't you just tell me what the dream means?"

He laughed his big booming laugh. "Mariah, I don't know what it means! Only you can discern what it means to you. I could make a guess, but--"

"Please," I interrupted. "I'd love to hear your guess."

Again he laughed, but then his voice grew soft. "This dream is too important. It wants *your* attention. That's why it's recurring. We can talk again, but first try what I suggest."

So I did. In fact, I made a bit of a ritual of it. I drank chamomile tea and ate two homemade ginger snaps. I meditated as my mother taught me to do, and I spoke to my dream as if it were a wise woman with knowledge to impart. Then I went to bed and slept.

The first two nights I had no dreams that I could recall. But on the third night what happened? I was given this tiny slice of cinnamon toast. Cinnamon toast! Beautiful but useless cinnamon toast! I felt so bad, it occurred to me I should plunk myself down in this familiar night hall and eat the damned toast myself!

That's when I woke up.

It was already morning, or so I thought. The room was well lit and sunlight appeared to be seeping through the closed blinds. I pulled my notebook from under my pillow to record the dream, because I like to do that in the morning. Admittedly, it's one of my quirkier hobbies. Anyway, I started to write, but I could barely keep my eyes open. Finally I happened to glance at the clock on my nightstand, and I was shocked: it said 2:15. Well, it certainly felt like 2:15 in the morning. I was so tired I could easily believe that it was still the middle of the night. But the light! Had I slept though breakfast and lunch? Could it possibly be 2:15 in the afternoon?

I noticed then that the room had a smoky quality to it. My white bedroom walls seemed tinged with a muted grey, and the blue and purple afghan on my bed looked soft yet vibrant, as if it were made of fancy cake frosting, buttery and shiny. Everything in the room looked that way, the dark cherry wood of my dresser, the ceramic vase filled with fresh yellow daisies I'd bought at the Farmers' Market. Everything had a velvety look, deeper, bigger, more rather than less real. The paper posters on my walls--the Georgia O'Keefe white morning glories, the Audubon blue and red tanagers--they didn't look flat anymore, they looked like thick and rich oil paintings, raised and imposing their vibrant colors on my eyes.

You might ask, I suppose, if I were still asleep, if I even wondered to myself if I might still be asleep. The answer is no, definitely not. I didn't even consider it. There is a particular quality to wakefulness, and there is a quality to dreams, just as there is to a state of meditation. All are different, and if you learn to pay attention you will not be easily confused.

And yet I was confused. My best guess was that there was something wrong with my alarm clock. I got up, left my bedroom and went into our dining room. All was how my roommate Rafa and I had left it the night before, when his new girlfriend had dined with us. Three used wine glasses still sat on the table, along with crumpled cocktail napkins--the ones I'd bought on sale at Mixed Bag a few weeks back. I bought them because the colors were so pretty, and it seemed a minor indulgence, these pretty little napkins with a mixture of fall fruits dashed across them in yellow and orange with a splash of dark purple. Now they sat crumpled up like little balls of melting color. They seemed to drip color, so shiny they glowed. In the kitchen, florescent dishes crowded the sink. Franciscan Country Apple handed down from my grandmother, now a blinding cream color with brittle red candied apples creating a throbbing border around the edge of each plate. The clock on the stove was brilliant yellow with red digits blaring out 2:23. It was now 2:23. Well, at least I knew my alarm clock hadn't stopped. But was it ante or post meridian? Still a mystery.

I crept on bare feet into the living room. I wanted to pound on Rafa's door, to ask straight out if the night had become a shining mass of color for him too, or whether it was mid afternoon. Maybe I would find him sitting at his desk, working on a biology term paper or pouring over a zoology textbook. But if it were still nighttime, I wouldn't want to disturb him. Gently I touched the doorknob and slowly, so slowly, turned it by tiny quarter inches. I peeked inside. Rafa was in his bed asleep with Jen. They lay with their backs to each other, a substantial gulf between them. Jen was snoring. Not loud, but loud enough.

I closed the door more quickly than I had opened it, feeling a little guilty that I'd caught a glimpse of such an intimate sight. Well, not exactly. I knew instantly that my guilt was coupled with, or perhaps caused by, a surprising feeling of smugness at the lack of intimacy I had observed. I told myself this was evidence of nothing, and that I didn't care anyway. I suddenly realized that I didn't much like Jen. Gee, I hadn't realized that before.

To clear these thoughts out of my mind I retreated to the front door, impulsively opened it and stepped out onto the balcony that runs the length of our second-story flat. There's an old leather couch that used to be white on the balcony. It was here when we moved in and it no doubt has been here for decades. I'm sure it was quite a fine couch when it was new, long and sleek and modern, rather Scandinavian looking. But it was covered with a dirty grey film, so I'd thrown an old but clean thrift store bedspread over it. It was a mild teal color with a tiny floral pattern, blossoms of salmon pink and lilac. I thought it looked quite attractive and Rafa agreed. We'd hung a few colorful tiles above it and the porch looked stylish and inviting. I stood out there now, swaying in the Northern California night air. It didn't look like night, but it felt like night, the air moist and cold, as if I'd stepped into a refrigerator. The street lights were lit, and when I looked up I was surprised to find the sky a deep and beautiful cobalt blue, filled with shimmering yellow, red and pale blue stars and planets. It took my breath away. I eased myself down onto the couch.

I hadn't washed the old bedspread in a month or more, and I became distracted by crumpled leaves and cobwebs that had settled in the folds between the cushions. It all seemed like flakes of gold dust or glitter. Yes, like glitter. I have to admit I got a little mesmerized fingering these bits of debris, glimmering like fairy dust, as if I'd fallen into Neverland, someplace mythical. I yawned. I was afraid if I didn't get up and move I might just fall asleep and the next thing I'd know it would be morning and here I'd be waking up on the porch in my pink peace sign T shirt and panties. I pulled myself to my feet, taking another quick look out at the familiar neighborhood: a creamy three story Victorian house with the majestic turret and the broad verandah, the ugly 1970s stucco apartment building, two 1920s bungalows flanking the alley. I swayed sleepily on my bare feet, my mind a blank.

Suddenly I saw a flat heart-shaped white disk drop down over the street, seemingly suspended on an invisible string. Huge yellow eyes stared at me. A disembodied face surged swiftly toward me as if carried by a river current. A stab of adrenaline hit my throat, then I realized this head was attached to majestic wings, beating with tremendous yet silent force. Unthinking, I crouched down and lifted my elbow to shield my face. It swooped toward me, then lifted at a sharp angle to sweep over and above our house. I rushed to the edge of the porch and looked upward trying to catch a glimpse of the bird as it sped west. Nothing. My heart was pounding in my chest and throat.

It was a barn owl, common enough, though I'd never seen one so close before. With my new night vision I'd been able to discern the downy white feathers of its belly ruffling in the breeze like the fine fronds of an asparagus fern. I was mesmerized but flustered, feeling I'd been visited by an apparition. My half-brother Dale is half Navajo, and he's told me barn owls are often called ghost owls by Native Americans. I had thought this was a whimsical nickname, but I understood now.

I was still having trouble catching my breath. It was only a bird, I told myself. A bird of prey, yes, but I'm too big for a bird that size to carry off. It was startling, that's all. Okay, I finally had to admit it, it scared the hell out of me, and I rushed back into the house.

I lifted my eyes to the ceiling. "Thank you, Universe," I whispered. "Once again you've proven yourself to be full of surprises!"

Then I went back to bed. It was nearly three by then, and I was still pretty tired. But it was hard to go back to sleep. My bedroom lights were off, my blinds were closed, but the light pounded on my eyelids as if I were trying to sleep on a sunny beach. Nonetheless, I did finally go back to sleep.

When I woke in the morning, the events of the two AM hour were not exactly forgotten, but I didn't concern myself with them. I had papers to write and books to read for my classes. I dressed, scarfed down a bowl of cereal and then rushed out to catch the light rail train to Sacramento State.

Chapter Two
Mariah's Journal

I spent the day on campus, going to classes, and studying in the library. My last class let out early evening, a little after six. It was starting to get dark out, but my eyes didn't sense the darkness. The sky was turning a richer deeper shade of blue. I hiked over to the light rail station, feeling like I had stepped into some kind of florescent Wonderland, a Peter Max painting or an old Disney cartoon. Cars and bushes, plants and trees, everything was taking on a jewel-toned glow. People's faces seemed to be emanating light. It felt dizzying to walk among these shimmering figures.

When I got home, Rafa was in the kitchen stir-frying garlic and onion, tofu and cauliflower. Rice was boiling on the stove. "Have you eaten yet?" he asked. "I've made plenty."

Rafa is capable in the kitchen though he views cooking as a utilitarian task, and his style is as pedestrian as a fry cook at a roadside truck stop. Eggs, burgers, onions and garlic, all tossed unceremoniously into a pan, along with whatever vegetable we've got wilting in the crisper. "Haven't you ever heard of a steamer?" I teased him as I entered the kitchen and nodded toward the mad sizzle and stench of vegetables bubbling in oil.

"Haven't you ever heard of the miracle of olive oil?" he announced in response. "Good for the heart, good for the arteries! It's a mono-unsaturated miracle! Miraculous olive oil!"

"Whaddya talking about?" I challenged. "Popeye's girlfriend?"

He laughed at my joke, probably grateful that I hadn't

berated him for his overuse of the word "miracle" again. I guess he's entitled; his life has been witness to more than his share of miraculous events. He told me once that "mystery," "miracle," and "magic," were among the first words he had learned in English. Not because he had asked for the "3m's" as he jokingly referred to this trinity, but because he heard them used so often in his household.

Rafael had been born in San Dismas, that tiny heart-shaped nation near the southern tip of Mexico. At least that's what the adoption agency was told. A woman identifying herself as his grandmother had sneaked across the border into Belize with him when he was a toddler. She abandoned him at a fire station in San Ignacio, telling the fire chief nothing but Rafa's first name and birth date.

Of course, Rafa remembers none of this. "They could tell me any story they want," he told me. "I'll believe it."

To Rafa, faith is a matter of practicality. He's happy to be here now, in a warm, dry, safe upper middle class existence, enjoying the privileges of an American life style. How he got here was a mystery. Anna, his adopted mom, has been told only snippets of a story, but she and my mom enjoy speculating and wondering. "You can write any story you want," Rafa always tells them. "Maybe they're all true. Doesn't matter to me. God brought me to my true family; that's all that matters."

I have to admit I'm curious about Rafa's origins, but I've had my own mysteries to contend with. When my mother was first pregnant with me twenty years ago, her doctors discovered she had a heterotopic pregnancy. That means she was pregnant with twins, but one of the zygotes was lodged in her left Fallopian tube. Luckily for me, I was the embryo that had made it into her uterus, and there I stayed safe and sound for the next nine months. But my twin had to be aborted when the tube was surgically removed--it was unavoidable--since mom's Fallopian tube was about to rupture, and of course that would have killed her.

My parents didn't tell me about my lost twin. In fact, maybe I never would have learned about him if my half-brother Dale hadn't let the story slip at the reception after our father's funeral. I was stunned, and yet it validated this feeling I'd always had that a piece of me was missing. A few months later, I met Rafa--and surprise! We have the same birth date! I know it sounds crazy, but I am convinced I've found my long-lost brother.

I've gotten used to eating Rafa's oily stir fries and he's happy to partake of the cookies and nut breads I like to turn out on a weekly basis. "Oh, you women!" he yells dramatically whenever I bring out another cake or pie. "You're gonna make me fat!" I endure his protests, though I know I am the one in graver danger from his overuse of olive oil. But Rafa was raised on the pies of his adopted mother, Anna Victoria, whose pie shops and business acumen are well known on two coasts. Rafa is none the worse from a life of eating sweets: he's six foot two and thin as a rail with a long lean face, peach fuzz on his chin and a mop of curly brown hair. He has long legs, long feet and long toes he likes to wiggle when he's thinking hard. Our friends say we will end up lovers, but we just laugh at that. We both know that our separate journeys have been riddled with complexity and paradox.

I cut up some pears and apples to mix with yogurt for a salad, and then set the table for us as Rafa finished up the stir-fry. He'd seasoned it with plenty of ginger. It tasted warm and comforting.

We chatted briefly about our classes, the weather, gossip, you know--small talk. Finally I said to him, "Do you notice anything different about the light?"

He looked up at the ceiling to the overhead lights. "Has a bulb gone out?" he asked. Seeing his motion, I automatically looked up too. Obviously this wasn't what I'd been talking about. "Somewhere else? In your bedroom?" he asked.

I smiled. I appreciated his concern. This old flat has high ceilings, and it's hard for me to reach the light fixtures. I have to put a couple textbooks on a chair for me to stand on when I need to change a light bulb. I much prefer that Rafa do that chore. "No, it's not a light bulb," I told him. I wasn't sure what to tell him. "Well, see, I had this dream--" I began.

"Oh, dream girl!" he interrupted in a sing-song teasing voice.

"Stop it," I protested with a laugh, but I didn't really mind. Rafa loves to tease me about my dreams. I love to write them down and talk about them. But Rafa claims he doesn't dream. I tell him that's impossible: everybody dreams. He just doesn't remember his dreams. He claims he's never ever remembered a dream, not a one. Sometimes he even seems a little proud of that fact. Other times I think he's fascinated when I tell him my dreams, maybe even a little jealous.

"What's the dream du jour?" Rafa asked with exaggerated interest.

I felt a little shy because it wasn't really the dream that I wanted to tell him about. It was a strange feeling because I never feel shy around Rafa. More than anybody else in the world, I can say what I think and feel to Rafa. But now I felt guarded, and I wasn't sure why. Maybe because the whole thing was just so darn crazy.

"Oh, it was that same dream I've been having for months now," I said lamely. "It's not very interesting."

Rafa raised his eyebrows. "You know, maybe that's the best attitude, Mariah. When you get bored with that dream, it'll probably go away."

I took a deep breath, still wondering at what message Craig

said the dream may have for me. "Maybe," I said in a noncommittal way as Rafa rose and began to clear the table.

"But then," I continued as I picked up a few dishes and followed him into the kitchen, "I woke up. It was two in the morning, and it was as light as day. I couldn't believe it. I walked out onto the porch and the sky was a deep blue color. It wasn't dark. I could see everything--the colors of the camellias and the cars. I even saw a big owl with a haunting heart-shaped face soaring toward me like a plane about to crash onto the porch."

Rafa started to fill the sink with water. "So," he said, "the dream did get pretty interesting. And a dream in color. Do you always dream in color? I've read most people dream in black and white."

"But that wasn't--" I began.

"You said the sky was deep blue, didn't you?" Rafa asked.

"Yes," I confirmed, and then I paused. I wanted to tell him that yes, he heard me right when I said the color of the sky. But I also wanted to point out that that wasn't a dream! I'd been awake when I saw the sky. I was awake now, I could go outside now, and see that same sky! Ever since I'd awakened at 2 AM the night before, my eyes had stopped seeing the darkness. My eyes saw nothing but light.

I stopped talking. I didn't want to tell him. I don't know why, but I didn't want to tell him. "You know," I said, faking a nonchalance I didn't feel, "I don't always remember if I dream in color or black and white. Sometimes I'll remember a vivid color, so I know that that particular dream was in color, but other times, if you'd ask me if it was color or black and white, I wouldn't know."

He nodded and turned toward the sink. "I'll do the dishes," I volunteered. He started to protest, but I told him it was only fair. "Sure, I know it's your turn, but you cooked dinner. Let me do the dishes."

He relented and I pushed back my sleeves. "You going out with Jen tonight?" I asked, but he said no.

"I don't think that's going anywhere," he said. "Plus--"

I jumped in to interrupt, and we said it in unison, "--she snores!"

We both laughed. We did that all the time. "That loud, huh?" he asked, looking a little embarrassed.

I laughed and turned to the dishes. Poor Jen, I thought. She really didn't snore that loud, but I didn't want to admit to Rafa that I'd peeked into his bedroom last night at 2:30. He probably wouldn't have cared, but I wasn't ready to share my weird secret yet.

Chapter Three
Rafa

Rafael Villasenor laid Mariah's notebook on her bedspread and rubbed his eyes.

He glanced at the clock on her nightstand. It was 2:15 AM. Funny, that was what she said in the notebook. She woke up and it was 2:15, but it was bright as day.

He swung his legs around and stood up in his stocking feet. He grabbed the notebook and brought it with him to the kitchen.   He opened the refrigerator, and found himself tempted to grab a bottle of beer. But no, that notebook was pretty damn thick; he still had an hour or more of reading ahead of him. He grabbed a couple of string cheese sticks that Mariah liked to carry in her backpack to snack on between classes. He took the cheese and the notebook to the living room and sprawled on the couch.

This little bit of effort sent his heart pounding again. He thought of Samantha, Mariah's mother, and knew she must be absolutely sick with worry. He opened the notebook again, hoping he'd find something in here that would provide a clue to Mariah's whereabouts.

Rafa hadn't seen Mariah in three and a half days. He hadn't worried at first, because--well, they both had different class schedules and sometimes life is like that. On Tuesdays and Thursdays he had an early morning biology lab, and sometimes he'd get up and leave before Mariah was up. On Monday evenings she had a film class, a class she was taking just for fun, she said. The professor was showing Shakespearean plays that had been adapted for the screen. Mariah said it was her favorite class, and it gave her three more English units. She was thinking she'd have enough for an English minor. But sometimes she'd go out with classmates for dessert or pizza-- whatever, and she wouldn't get home till late, and then she and Rafa might not see each other at all. So see, that was why he didn't worry at first. Of course they usually spoke on the phone or texted each other. Every day, they did that. He should have realized something was wrong when she didn't respond to his texts. He should have picked up on this sooner.

Mariah's half-brother Dale had told Rafa not to blame himself. Dale was a lawyer seventeen years Mariah's senior. He was very action-oriented. He didn't believe in wasting time on worry or regret. Move forward, he often told Rafa and Mariah, or less gently: *Get over it!* Wallowing and whining were a waste of time.

Still Rafa had felt bad when he went to the police station with Dale and Samantha. Her mother and brother had told the police sergeant over and over again that this disappearance was out of character for Mariah, that Mariah was a good girl, that she would never go anywhere or do anything without telling her family, without telling Rafa her roommate, who was just like a brother to her.

Rafa suddenly felt bad, chewing on the string cheese, a small circle of anxiety pulsing in his throat and solar plexus. "Just like a brother," Samantha had told the police officer. She'd said it two times, maybe three. "Just like." He couldn't expect anyone else to understand. It wasn't "just like." It was exactly. It was actual. It was real. He was Mariah's brother. Mariah was his sister. Yes, they had different parents, but that was an accident. They were brother and sister as sure as Dale was Mariah's brother and Luisa was Rafa's sister. Mariah and Rafa were related. The two of them were sure of it.

Rafa pulled his cell phone from his pocket and with a few quick taps brought up a photo of Mariah he had taken last summer when they went swimming with friends at Folsom Lake. The police had wanted a picture and Rafa had wanted to give them this one, but Samantha had one she liked better.

Rafa slumped back on the couch and stared at his phone. Mariah had a look on her face so sincere it was almost comical. She was sipping soda or lemonade through a straw, staring with open curiosity, listening to someone at her immediate right. She looked like a girl in a magazine ad, a girl so wholesome you'd want to go out and fight a war to preserve her honor. Rafa couldn't remember who Mariah had been looking at that day, but at least once a week, he'd bring the photo up just so he could look at her. Sometimes her expression made him laugh, but always it gave him a warm feeling--maybe you'd call it affection—a feeling of comfort, even security, knowing she was his best friend.

He leaned forward. He never thought about it much, but he couldn't help but notice that Mariah was a pretty girl. In this photo, he knew her hair was damp since she'd been swimming, but it was still lovely: long and thick, the color of clover honey. Her eyes were dark brown. And now for the first time he noticed that the two-piece swim suit she wore did nothing to hide the fullness of her breasts. He drew a quick breath. When they'd met two years ago, Mariah had been small and thin, typical of many teenaged girls. But Mariah had developed womanly curves in a very short time. Why hadn't Rafa noticed? He flipped off his phone. Maybe this was why Samantha preferred another photo.

He picked up the notebook again, and rifled through its pages. The midnight snack had done nothing to alleviate the guilt he felt for having lied at the police station. He meekly agreed when Samantha had described Mariah as a sweet girl who would never engage in any kind of behavior that could even remotely be described as reckless. But lately--well, there were things Rafa could have said, things he should have said, but he didn't want to say these things in front of Samantha. He didn't want to upset her any more than she already was.

When they were leaving the station, Rafa had pulled Dale

aside. "I need to talk to you," he'd whispered to Dale.

Dale nodded, thinking. "Look, let me call you in the morning. I've got to take Samantha home." Rafa nodded. He knew Dale was very protective of his stepmother and half-sister. His late father had made him promise to look after them. Rafa's sister Luisa was Dale's partner, and she often teased Dale, saying he saw himself as a border collie patrolling the perimeter of the ranch. Dale would protest, but everybody else in the family thought it was funny. Nonetheless, they were grateful for the role he'd taken on. Rafa nodded. "Okay, tomorrow then."

"Are you okay?" Dale asked, apparently realizing Rafa was another sheep to look after. "You can come over to our house tonight if you want, stay with me and Luisa."

"No, no, I'm fine," Rafa assured him. "Besides, I think I should be at our apartment, you know, in case Mariah comes home."

"Oh! You're right--and you know what?--she probably will," Dale said. "You know I've got a very bad tendency to always expect the worse, but you're right. She'll probably just come home."

"Hope so," Rafa said.

"And I don't want you blaming yourself," Dale said for the third or fourth time. "We've got to move forward."

Move forward, Rafa thought. Right. So he drove right home, strode into Mariah's bedroom and started searching for notebooks. He knew Mariah had suddenly begun keeping a diary a month or so ago. Journaling, she called it. There had to be a clue or two in here someplace.

Chapter Four
Mariah's Journal

My godfather came to the flat to visit me. I was surprised because he'd only been to my flat once before and he came with my mother that time.

Craig is a big man, barrel-chested and balding. On this day he was wearing a pale brown T-shirt with a swirling Asian dragon silk-screened onto it. I invited him in and we sat at the dining room table. We ate trail mix and red flame grapes. I offered him herbal tea but he wasn't interested in that. My mother always said he was a meat and potatoes kind of guy, despite all the spiritual stuff he espoused. He didn't drink anything but soda, fully leaded, none of that diet crap. Unfortunately I had no sugary drinks to offer him.

He asked me if I'd still been having the dream about the hungry children. "Oh, no," I said, surprised to realize that I'd forgotten about my dream what with everything else going on. "I had the dream one more time since I talked to you, but not in the past week." I shrugged. "Maybe it's fading away, but I still don't know what it means."

He smiled. "Your heart has many ways to talk to you. Whatever you need to know will come to you when the time is right."

After a bit more small talk about my classes and my friends, Craig pulled a stack of notebooks out of his backpack. He said he brought them to me as a present. They weren't anything special, just some college-ruled, spiral-bound notebooks. I thanked him sincerely, since he seldom gave presents, and then--to be polite--I told him these note books would come in handy for my classes, because I liked to take a lot of notes. And I like to take notes in long hand, rather than on a laptop. That's kind of rare these days.

Craig leaned forward then and tapped the blue notebook on the top of the stack. "These notebooks aren't for your university classes," he told me.

I raised my eyebrows, unsure of how to respond, so I waited. He smiled.

"You have something to write down," he said simply. "It's time for you to do that."

I leaned back in my chair. "I have something to write down?" I repeated in a quizzical tone. I looked up at him, but he only nodded. "What do you mean?"

He laughed. He has this amazing smile; his whole face crinkles into laugh lines. "Well, I don't know," he said innocently. "Maybe you don't know either! But if you don't know now, wait a while. You'll know soon. Soon you will have something to write. You'll know when it happens."

I was stunned. My mother always said that Craig was psychic, though he himself disavowed the word. She had told me that Craig's clairvoyance had guided her often when she was younger, and once it even saved her life. I had to admit that I'd seen little evidence of this "psychic gift" over the years. When I had pointed this out to my mother, she told me that I hadn't seen Craig use his gift because I hadn't needed him to use his gift for me. Whatever. But now--well, maybe there was something to this psychic stuff.

"Mariah," Craig was saying, "you don't have to tell me what it is you have to write about; you don't have to tell anybody. But when the time comes--and you'll know it when it does-- write it down."

"And then I should give you the notebook?" I asked him.

"Oh, no, that's not necessary," he said quickly. He took another handful of granola, and picked out a few raisins to discard. "Of course you can if you want to, but the point is to write. There is no other goal. Just write."

I stared at him as he tossed the granola into his mouth and chewed. "Do you want these raisins?" he asked nonchalantly.

"No," I said. "Thank you."

We sat in silence for a few minutes as he continued to eat. I stared out the window. It was late afternoon. Within a half hour the sun would be setting and again the world would turn into a soft and bright place, with deep colors and no darkness. It had been five nights since my eyes had been unable to detect darkness, and the situation was wearing on me. I'd gone down to Mixed Bag and found myself one of those sleep masks so I could create an artificial darkness when I wanted to sleep at night. I felt hyper and unrested. The whole thing was weird and I hadn't talked to anyone about it yet.

"Craig," I said slowly.

"mmm, hmmm," he murmured.

"I want to show you something," I said. "Out on the porch."

We went out to our balcony and sat on the old leather sofa. I pointed at the leaves of the sycamore tree in the dusky light. "What color would you say those leaves are?" I asked him.

He squinted. "It's hard to say in this light," he said. "I'm guessing they're yellow or maybe light brown right now. But I'm also guessing there's a bigger reason why you're asking me this. I don't think you care so much what color I think the leaves are."

"My mom always said you were a psychic," I told him.

"Well, your mom likes her drama and mystery sometimes," he said with a laugh. "I'm not a psychic. I just see what's there for anyone to see. If they're paying attention." He paused. "And what are you seeing, Mariah?"

I pursed my lips, anxious about revealing my crazy secret. "What I'm seeing," I said, "is everything!"

We ordered a large pizza with pineapple and Canadian bacon and a six-pack of Dr. Pepper. We sat eating in the dining room and I told him about my dream and how I woke up at two AM, and the apartment and the street and the garden were bright as day. I told him how the world became velvety and deep at night, but never dark. I told him how I'd decided it was easiest to hide in my bedroom and cover my eyes in the evening, because I didn't like thinking about it.

"Why is this happening?" I asked him.

"I don't know," he said.

"But if you don't know--"

"Not much of a psychic now, am I?" he said with a loud snort and self-deprecating laugh.

I looked at him in frustration. Maybe I shouldn't have trusted him at all. He leaned forward and tapped my hand. "Look," he said, his voice low, suddenly serious. "Let's call this new ability of yours a gift. Maybe you'll learn to see it that way, and maybe you won't, but let's assume it's a gift."

He paused to help himself to more pizza. "Okay," I said, "but--"

He held up a hand. "Hold on," he said, "let me finish." He took another bite. "You see," he continued, "we humans are always asking why. Sometimes the why is easy to figure out, sometimes it's not. Sometimes we make up an answer just to

satisfy our curiosity. The fact is there's only one reason why--
and that's energy. We are led to go where we go and do what
we do by energy. The energy doesn't care about the story you
want to create. The energy just is. And the energy will work
through you whether you cooperate with it or not. But one
thing is certain: if you want to know why you've been given
this gift, then you have to use it. You can't sit in your room and
cover your eyes and hope it's gone when you wake up."

"What do you mean--use it?" I asked. "I can't help but 'use
it' when my eyes are open. It just happens, I can't control it."

"It seems to me," Craig said, fingering his slice of pizza,
"that a gift like yours intends for you to see something in the
dark. Something that's normally hidden in the darkness. But
I'm guessing here."

I sat silent for a moment, and honestly I felt rather sullen.
Was he saying I should go out in the dark, looking around in
corners and shadows? Just looking? That didn't feel very safe.
Didn't he have any concern for my safety?

He swallowed his pizza, and took a sip of Dr. Pepper. "You
are always protected, Mariah," he said softly. "The universe
would not lead you someplace to endanger you. Don't worry
about that."

He had read my mind! He knew what I was thinking as
easily as if I'd spoken it aloud. I took a deep breath; I felt
violated.

"Could you always do that?" I asked him. "I mean have you
always been doing that? Reading my mind all along?"

"What?" He seemed startled. "No, of course not. I don't
read minds. That would be rude. You know, like peeking
through people's windows or something."

"But you just---"

"If it seemed I read your mind, Mariah," Craig said, "it was inadvertent. I don't deliberately read anybody's mind. But the information comes to me when I need it--or when you need me to have it. If you were worrying about your safety, you wanted me to know that. Or else I wouldn't know that."

I felt humbled by his explanation. I sat quietly staring at my empty plate, my hands in my lap. My mother always said that Craig was here on earth in servitude to the Divine Essence. Of course he had no intention of spying on me. I glanced meekly up at him, but he seemed unconcerned, munching on more pizza. I took a deep breath.

"You think I should wander around outside at night, 'using' this gift?" I asked, hoping I didn't sound too challenging.

He laughed. "Mariah, I don't think you should do anything. You wanted to know why this is happening to you, and I'm suggesting that the only way to find out is to use the gift. That doesn't mean you need to do anything out of the ordinary. Just go about your life. When my daughters were in their teens and twenties, they were barn owls, wanting to go out all the time, wanting to explore. If you're anything like they were, you'll have ample opportunity to try out this new super power you have."

"'Barn Owls?'" I said in surprise, remembering the bird I'd seen aiming at our porch that first night.

"Yeah," he said uncertainly. "Oh, the expression is 'Night Owl,' huh? I guess I meant to say Night Owls." He shrugged as he poured himself more soda. "You know what I mean."

I nodded. "Yeah," I said softly, but my mind was racing. I remembered what my mother had told me about Craig and his abilities. "He's not what you'd think a psychic would be," she'd told me. "He's not on stage, offering to make contact with your dead uncle or to guess what color you're thinking about. There are things he just knows."

Craig put down his soda and I glanced over at him again. "Look, Mariah," he said in a boisterous voice. "My best advice-- under any circumstance--is to follow the energy. Pay attention: the universal energy is guiding you. You will discern it. You just have to quiet all the traffic in your mind, and pay attention."

I stared at him and nodded, wondering if it would really be this easy.

"Your mother," he continued. "She's done a pretty good job over the years of following the energy. Sometimes she gets distracted, but she knows what she's doing." He paused as if deciding whether to continue. "Your father--well, he let the energy lead him all over the place. It seemed he had a hard time discerning which energy belonged to him. He had a lot of traffic in his head."

I stared at Craig. I loved my father, and was happy to be getting new, clearer perspectives on who he was. Right away I knew Craig was right. Too much traffic.

"And then," Craig continued, "don't forget to write it all down."

I stood up. This was too much. He was being deliberately mysterious and it was annoying the hell out of me. "Tell me why," I demanded. "I want to know why you want me to keep a journal."

He grimaced as if embarrassed. "I can't do that Mariah," he said, and I squealed in frustration. He shook his head. "It's not that I don't want to tell you; it's that I don't know! I'm following the energy too. It's what I do. The idea came to me that you would be a writer over two years ago. And two weeks ago, after you told me about your dream, I realized that you needed a push. I sat on that thought for a while, but it resonated with me, gained energy. I knew I had to come see you."

He looked at me with a small smile, testing for my reaction. He lifted his hands. "That's how it works," he concluded. "That's how I live my life."

Rafa came through the door then and we offered him the rest of the pizza. Rafa and I shared a beer, and Craig drank another can of soda. I brought out some lemon bars I'd made over the weekend and Craig loved them. He ate three. Rafa told him about the biology classes he was taking, and about how he hoped to transfer to the veterinarian program at UC Davis in a few years.

"And what about you, Mariah?" Craig asked. "Have you focused on a career goal yet?"

I felt my cheeks color a bit. I was embarrassed that even as I started my second year of college I hadn't decided on a major or settled on what I wanted to do when I graduate. I smiled awkwardly and Rafa jumped in to save me. "Mariah's still exploring," he said, and I gave him a grateful glance.

"I'm taking lots of different classes," I said. "But I'm thinking that eventually I'll become a social worker or a nurse, or maybe a teacher like my Mom."

"Well," he said, as he helped himself to another lemon bar, "if you decide to open a bakery, you've got my endorsement."

I was happy to have Craig stay late and talk with Rafa and me. If Craig hadn't been here, Rafa might have gone to his room to study, or left to meet yet another girl. As it was, we were all here, sitting in bright light after moving to the living room, and I didn't have to notice the lack of darkness. At one point Rafa got up to clear the dishes and carry them to the kitchen. When he started back through the dining room, I called to him to remember to turn off the kitchen light. "I did turn it off," he said. "Just now."

"Oh," I said, feeling a little uneasy that my secret had almost been caught out. Craig looked at me expectantly. I think he was surprised that I hadn't told Rafa. But I'm not ready. Not yet.

Chapter Five
Rafa

Rafa woke up on the couch, Mariah's notebook on his chest. The clock on the wall was nearing six AM though it was still rather dark in the room.

Rafa wasn't sure what to make of this mysterious ability to see in the dark that Mariah was talking about in her notebook. Still he wasn't all that surprised. History was replete with numerous examples of men and women who had developed special skills and abilities. Well, Catholic history anyway. In his twelve years of Catholic education, Rafa had had a full exposure to the lives of saints, mystics, desert ascetics, and innocent children with spectacular visions. And yet few of them could even hold a candle to his older sister, Luisa.

Anna had adopted Luisa from the same international agency where she'd found Rafa--only 14 years earlier. Luisa had appeared to be a healthy baby, but it soon became apparent that she was showing symptoms of autism spectrum disorder. She had in fact very severe stereotypic behaviors. She appeared to be trapped in a world of self-stimulation: rocking, waving her fingers in front of her face, banging her head against the wall and the floor, crying and wetting herself. She appeared to have severe cognitive disabilities, destined for a life requiring complete care, perhaps even institutionalization.

Luisa was 11 years old when she was enrolled in Mariah's mother's special education class. With Anna's insistent encouragement, Samantha was able to draw Luisa out with a technique called facilitated communication. Luisa learned to type independently to communicate. She revealed herself to be an intelligent and vibrant young woman. With the support of instructional assistants, and adapted assessment instruments,

Luisa was able to earn degrees in philosophy and comparative religions. She held a PhD. from Princeton, and was employed as a part-time faculty member, teaching online classes, at Yale. She was still unable to speak, but she conveyed her intelligence, her humor and her complex personality with the assistance of robotic devices.

Growing up in a home with Luisa, coupled with the teaching of the nuns, led Rafa to believe that the miraculous was commonplace. Didn't everyone have a saint or two in his family? As a child, he'd even brought Luisa to school for show and tell. "This is my sister, the miracle," he introduced her. He was disappointed to learn that no one else had a saint, a miracle or perhaps a fairy godmother or two living in their households. He was even more surprised to discover that the other children were more intrigued with the Star Wars quality machines with robotic voices that helped Luisa communicate than they were with Luisa herself. Didn't they realize she was an advanced spiritual being? Didn't they get it?

Learning that Mariah had some kind of new super power gave Rafa a great sense of relief. Somehow this restored the natural balance. This was how the world was supposed to work. Miracles weren't supposed to be hidden or explained away. Yes, they surprise, they delight. They often inconvenience, and even scare you. But they are here and now, and as ordinary as salt.

What did surprise Rafa was the casual way Mariah described her godfather. Rafa had been excited to meet a girl who had known Craig all her life, who had been baptized with Craig as her godfather. Maybe it was the familiarity that blunted her awe. Or maybe she'd never been told. Why wouldn't her parents, Samantha and Charlie, tell Mariah that Craig was a Perfect Master? Certainly Samantha knew. She had seen Samantha joke with Craig; she didn't seem deferential at all. And yet, Luisa had told him that Samantha had a deep reverence for Craig and honored him as her guide. It was perplexing.

Rafa glanced over at the clock again. It was just past 6:30, and he could barely keep his eyes open. Surely it was too early to call Dale. He picked up the notebook and began again to read.

Chapter Six
Mariah's Journal

After Craig left and Rafa went to his room to study, I told Rafa I was going to make a Ben and Jerry's run. I certainly wasn't lying, but instead of taking my car I walked. First I went up to K Street, and I strolled along past the closed shops and galleries. It was well past nine o'clock and the lights were dimmed most everywhere, but it didn't matter. I could see everything. Even the tiniest little earrings in the jewelry store were blazing stars to my new eyes. I could see the newly hung Halloween decorations: pumpkins, cats and scarecrows. I found a pair of navy blue running shoes in the Diesel store window. They had lime green laces with little bits of gold glitter at the tips. New leather purses for fall in green and orange, and black canvas tote bags with sunflowers splashed across them. It was fun to know I was the only one who could see these beautiful items sitting in the shop windows, everything looking soft and pliable like brilliantly colored bread dough. I approached Rick's Dessert Diner and there were people out on the street in the September chill sitting at little café tables eating massive slices of dark chocolate cakes and florescent white and yellow cheese cakes. So pretty. The people themselves were shiny, laughing and chatting in loud voices. I was surprised to feel exhilarated by their energy. Their energy! It's as if I could see thin bands of gold and silver light flowing from the tops of their heads and the palms of their hands. I wondered that I hadn't noticed it before. I knew I was gaping, and I tried to subdue myself, but then I realized that I was in the shadow of a nearby shop, and they couldn't see me. How convenient this gift is, I realized. I could freely observe, noticing that the waves of light were sometimes red, sometimes blue or green, even orange or pink. It was subtle, I had to squint to see it, but oh--so beautiful!

I hurried on down the street past Tres Hermanas, still crowded with people too, but not many on the street outside. I glanced at my cell phone to check the time. It was nearing ten, and I had an early class in the morning. I better head back. But first I rounded the corner to pass in front of St. Francis of Assisi Church where Rafa and I attend mass on weekends. There on the steps was a knot of homeless people bedding down for the night. I knew they welcomed the homeless there, but I had never been by at this hour to see them. The steps were very crowded, still I was grateful they had a place to stay. I started to avert my eyes; I didn't want to invade their privacy. But there in the corner near the side door, a middle-aged gentleman with graying hair and a neatly trimmed beard sat cross-legged, staring at me as I came up the street. He was in the shadows, but of course I could see him. The darkness of shadows paradoxically makes faces and objects appear deeper and richer in my eyes, and it seemed to me this man's features were sculpted from a very fine silk. His nose was too big and his hairline was receding, but he had a long thin face and high cheekbones. He looked quite beautiful there on the steps, his face a bit pinched in the night air, his lips pressed together in what looked like worry. His eyes never left my face, and I was unable to look away too, although I kept walking closer and closer. Finally I gave a quick nod of acknowledgement and raised my hand in greeting--you know, just to be polite. He looked stunned; he obviously had been unaware that I could see him. I felt bad as if I had committed some great social faux pas. After all, here on these steps, at this hour, this man is in his bedroom. I felt like a peeping tom. I lowered my head and hurried past.

I stopped at the Mom and Pop store at the corner of 24th and N. They didn't have Cherry Garcia ice cream, but they had a variety of other Ben and Jerry flavors to sample. I chose Phish Food. That would do.

Chapter Seven
Rafa

Rafa yawned in frustration. There was nothing in this notebook to indicate where Mariah might be. He was shivering now, and he knew it wasn't because he was cold. I'm scared, he admitted to himself as he leafed through the next few pages.

He sighed. Why the hell didn't she date any of this stuff? How was he supposed to know when any of this had happened?

What followed in the notebook were quick descriptions of trips out with friends to downtown cafes and dance clubs. He knew she'd been going out nearly every night. It had begun to worry him. Three times now he'd met her coming into the flat in the morning just as he was headed off to class. And all three times, he couldn't help but notice that she wasn't wearing her bra. He wanted to ask her about it, but he didn't dare. A couple times she'd come home wearing heavy goth make-up, and once she was all steam punk with a felt top hat, a ruffled shirt, and high buttoned boots. She said she'd borrowed the costume from somebody and she'd be returning it that night. The worst was the night she came home at midnight with a bruise on her cheek. Rafa thought he'd jump out the window to go find whoever had done that to her.

"Calm down, Rafa," she'd drawled, laying a warm hand on his chest and leaving it there. "It's make-up, see?" She licked her thumb, and swiped it roughly across her face. "See?" she repeated, holding up her appendage to show off the purple and brown paint. "I've just been on my first zombie walk!" Her eyes looked a little dazed, and she smelled of weed.

"What have you been doing?" Rafa blurted in a loud and

frantic tone, but Mariah was obviously too sleepy to comprehend his panicked concern. "What is going on with you lately?"

Then his girlfriend of the moment, Angie, who had been observing this exchange from across the room, suddenly got up and strutted between them, a little girl demanding her share of the attention. "I need to get going," she said in a husky stage whisper. "You coming?"

Rafa stuffed his hands into his pockets, suddenly so angry that he wanted to push her aside. "I'll call you tomorrow," he said sharply.

"Don't bother," Angie hissed. She sashayed to the door, somehow making her flat sandals sound like stilettos. It was an eerie effect. Made him pause to wonder how she'd done it. And thus distracted, he missed how Mariah had snuck out of his sight and into the bathroom. He had lingered at the door for a moment, but Mariah was in the shower. He had gone to bed.

He turned the pages of the notebook, looking over a slap dash record of the past month or so. Parties at classmates' apartments, drinking with a fake ID at bars down near the Capitol, pub crawls and the infamous zombie walk. All he knew was that she was seldom home anymore. But when did that begin? Late September? Early October? He studied a paragraph about going to Tower Café with Rafa and his new girlfriend Bobbie. Rafa drummed his hand on the notebook. He'd gone out with Bobbie for no more than a week and a half. But when was that? It was after Jen, and before Angie, right? He stood up and strode into the kitchen. Yeah, Angie was after Bobbie, because it was Angie that had introduced him to Renee. He was going to call Renee and break up with her right now. Well, later today, or maybe he'd wait till tomorrow.

He opened the refrigerator, and was again tempted to grab

a beer for breakfast. That wouldn't go over very well with Dale. And Dale would know; Dale could just tell. That was his super power. He was usually cool about it. "Find somebody else to drive tonight," he'd say in a low voice when he smelled alcohol or marijuana on Rafa's clothes. Or he'd say, "Call me if you need to." He was the perfect surrogate big brother. He'd have made a great father. But he and Luisa had decided against that.

Rafa grabbed Mariah's carton of cottage cheese. He didn't feel like going to all the effort of frying eggs or pancakes. A day without butter and vegetable oil, he thought as he dished up the cottage cheese and sliced a pear on top of it. Maybe he could do a modified Lenten fast to please the ascetic Desert Saints, convince them to forgive his lack of attention, his hedonistic explorations, and then Mariah would come home.

He took his breakfast bowl to the living room and sprawled again on the couch with the blue notebook. He turned the page and found a list of names, men's names. Each one had been assigned a number. He nearly choked on a chunk of pear. He turned the page quickly, not wanting to speculate on what this list might mean. He chewed his food carefully, thought about returning to the kitchen to make coffee. Then he put down his bowl and picked up the notebook again. He took a deep breath to steel himself, then turned back to the list. He counted. Seven names. Seven. That wasn't so bad, though she certainly accumulated that list awfully fast. Maybe this wasn't what he thought. He put the book down again. He grabbed his jacket and headed out to buy an espresso.

Chapter Eight
Mariah's Journal

When I was in high school I gave myself to a boy named Todd. I wasn't in love, though I guess I liked him well enough. At the time I have to admit that I didn't think about it much. It was toward the end of junior year in high school, I had just turned seventeen, and I decided it was time. As if losing one's virginity is some kind of developmental milestone. Oh, well. All of my friends had paired up and they were doing it. I thought why not, guess I better find somebody too. Todd seemed interested. He offered me his class ring and his letter jacket. I know. I'm making it sound like it was a trade of some kind. At the time I felt he offered me those things as a sign of commitment. But later I realized he was branding me.

The sex itself was not very creative. There was no oral action below the neck. None! What can I say, Todd wasn't a very creative person. He was on the basketball team, second string. He had a great three-point shot. If the rest of the team worked the defense just right and got him open, he nearly always hit it. So that's mainly what he'd do in a game, hang around the three-point line, waiting. Just waiting. See what I mean--not very creative. But when he'd score, he'd score big, and the crowd would go wild.

He was a jock and very good looking. Brown hair, blue eyes, solid jaw and high cheek bones. Looks count for a lot in high school. I have to admit I was as shallow as the next girl when it came to that.

He liked sports of course. He liked to come over on Sundays and watch football or basketball games with Daddy. That earned him points. Mom and I would bake cookies or pie, and we'd order pizza. It was fun. It wasn't till later that I realized that I had more fun baking with my mom and watching basketball with my Dad when Todd wasn't there. Ironic, huh?

I broke up with him almost immediately after my father died. That was senior year.

The following year, I didn't want to go back to school. I stayed with my mother. We traveled. Sometimes Dale came with us. Anna, Luisa, and Rafa moved to California, and we had happy times helping them settle into their new homes. Of course, shortly thereafter, Luisa decided to move in with Dale, and Rafa and I rented this flat. Mom and Anna bought houses near each other in River Park. "The new normal," Mom called it. "No, it's new adventures," I told her. She looked a little sad, and guilty that she was making me sad too. I'm sure she felt like she was putting a damper on my new adventures, the decisions I was making to move my life forward. I just don't want her to think that her life is over now that Daddy is gone. She can have new adventures too. It will take a while for her to find them.

Chapter Nine
Samantha

Samantha sat up and pulled the cord to turn on the overhead light. She struggled to get out of bed: her lower back ached and her feet hurt. Some mornings she felt like she'd been running in her dreams, running, in fact, without adequate arch support. But not last night. There had been no dreams last night because there had been no sleep. And yet these vulnerable feet felt worn and abused anyway.

As she rose she caught a glimpse of herself in the mirror. She had gotten her perennially long hair cut a mere month after the sudden death of her husband in what she later admitted was a kind of grief frenzy. The severe pixie cut was one of those bad decisions grief counselors warn you about. In the intervening two years, Samantha's hair had grown into a chin length bob that Mariah had declared flattering. Still a good hair cut could not hide the worry lines around her mouth and eyes.

She checked her cell phone that sat on top of her dresser. Nothing. She expected nothing, since after all, she'd left the phone set on "loud" all night. And since she hadn't slept, she surely would have heard if a call had come in. Still, she hoped. It was a compulsive urge, an unrelenting habit--this hope. Sometimes she still looked out the window, hoping she might see Charlie coming up the walk, smelling of wood smoke and fennel. He had been the adventurer, not her. He was always seeking some new sensation, a new taste or smell or sound--or even some new emotion. She got the feeling sometimes that he experimented with different arguments, different intellectual postulates in order to evoke new feelings, both in himself and in Samantha. He'd suggest moving back east to the woods of New Hampshire, for example, as if he wanted to see how she would react. More than once he quit his job suddenly, without talking to her about it, and then there was the time he announced that he was leaving to hike the Pacific Crest Trail, and he didn't expect to return for ten to twelve weeks. "Yes," he would agree when she told him it was selfish and unreasonable of him, "but how does it make you feel? Really get into that emotion! See where it leads you!"

She half expected one of these days that he would slide through the door as if nothing had happened, as if he weren't really dead, just hiding, and when she greeted him with joy, relief, and some anger too, he would say, "And what was it like for you, you know--emotionally? Did you break through any walls with that feeling? Knock down any barriers? Cross through to a new dimension perhaps?"

Mariah, the only offspring of their union, had been surprisingly level-headed. She showed no signs of inheriting Charlie's quirky impulsiveness, nor Samantha's obsessive perfectionism. She was a mellow child, easily excelling at school--just as both her parents had--but she seemed unattached to this success. She didn't let it define her. Samantha felt both blessed and surprised that her daughter created so little drama, particularly since her husband created so much.

But since her father's death, Mariah seemed to pick up where Charlie left off. During a road trip they'd taken shortly after Charlie's death, Mariah became separated from Samantha and Dale--well actually she'd left them and taken off on her own. But at least that time she'd kept in touch by cell phone. They knew pretty much where she was. Now--well, Samantha didn't know what to think. This was not Mariah.

As soon as Rafa called her and Dale to say that Mariah had been missing, Samantha contacted her friend Craig. She sent him an email and left a message on his voice mail. Craig never answered the phone and seldom spoke on it at all. But he called Samantha within a half hour. "Mariah is safe," he announced without prelude as soon as Samantha picked up the phone.

"How do you know?" she fired back.

"Samantha," he said simply.

She gnawed on her upper lip. Samantha had known Craig for over three decades and had seen numerous examples of his clairvoyant abilities. Many's the times he'd arrived at the house she shared with her husband and then let slip he was aware that she and Charlie had spent the previous evening blissfully reading poetry to each other, or that they'd been fighting like cats and dogs. He was always right.

Another time she saw Craig walk into the school library and head directly to a shelf where he picked out the book that had the answers Samantha sought. "How did you do that?" she asked. He had shrugged. "The book called me over," he said.

But she would never forget the day Craig had told her she was pregnant with Mariah. Samantha had been told so many times by so many fertility experts that she was sterile that she hadn't wanted to believe Craig. She couldn't stand the thought of getting her hopes up only to be dashed again. But thankfully he had been right, and thus began the happiest journey of her life.

He had proved his understanding of universal energy time and time again. Why was she scared to believe him now?

She stared blankly out her front window, waiting as she was for Dale to come pick her up so they could go fill out the police report. She had wanted to drive down to the station and meet Dale there, but Dale had been insistent. How did Charlie manage to raise such a responsible young man? She was blessed to have him as a stepson.

She released an exasperated sigh into her cell phone. "I need to know more," she said decisively. "What do you even mean by *safe?* My daughter may have dropped dead but that's fine with you because her spirit is safe and sound on the astral plane somewhere."

"Samantha," he said again, but this time her name held a scolding tone, a plea for reason.

But Samantha would not apologize. She spoke slowly, barely breathing lest she burst into tears. "I'm so scared, Craig."

"I know," he said somberly. "I'm sorry this is so hard on you. But please trust me. You'll hear from Mariah soon."

"Are you sure? Tonight? Will it be tonight?"

"I don't know, Samantha, but I don't think it will be tonight."

"Jesus, Craig!" she exclaimed. "What's your idea of soon?"

"Ye-ah," he drawled as if embarrassed. "I was hoping you wouldn't ask that."

Then Dale had driven up and she'd gotten off the phone. Yet she'd held on to this stupid hope for the past 18 hours, chanting Craig's words in her head and heart: Mariah is safe, Mariah is safe.

She had to wonder if this relentless feeling of panic would indeed launch her into a new dimension, some mystical plane of existence perhaps--or if it would kill her. Craig always said that each of us chooses what we will experience before we are born, or as Craig put it, before we enter the human vehicle. Maybe it's true, Samantha thought, maybe it's not. If she had chosen this, then she better figure out fast what it was she was supposed to learn from it, and then Mariah would come home. Would that work? She didn't really think so.

She fed the cat and then got dressed. She checked her phone again, making sure it had a sufficient charge. Then she went out for a walk along the levee. The sun was playing along the rushing current of the river, flashing green, yellow and brown reflections in the water. The river looked swift, but then Samantha caught sight of two fishermen wading out with their poles. They planted themselves in the center, and the water line hit them no higher than mid-calf. How low that rushing current was! She was reminded again that the previous year had been dangerously dry. She wondered what was in store for them now.

Chapter Ten
Mariah's Journal

It's been an interesting few weeks. I've been out nearly every night, by myself or with friends, and it's been--uh, hmmmm.

I was going to say it's been fun, but fun isn't the right word. I was going to say interesting, but I don't want to be redundant. It's been work. I feel like an anthropologist, studying the nocturnal habits of early 21st century, information age young adults, with a focus on urban American middle class college students. Yessir, does this girl know how to lay on the academic term paper lingo or what? Maybe I'll never land on a career path, but I'm well equipped to spend my life writing one term paper after the other. Whatev.

In the last two weeks, I've been to parties, dance clubs, bars, art exhibit openings, concerts and a poetry reading. This flurry of social activity has afforded me the opportunity to uh-- I was going to say experiment, but let's face it, it's given me ample opportunity to hook up.

I'd been refusing all offers, but the other night, a guy from my Shakespeare film class was suddenly there, and I decided to take a chance. It wasn't something I'd planned or anything, it just seemed to happen. I was at a party given by a woman in that same class. I had stationed myself at a butcher-block table in the corner of the kitchen. I was off to the side, but I still had a clear view of the front door so I could people watch. It was loud, there was a keg, and people were streaming in from God knows where. I wondered if Mattie--the woman giving the party—I wondered if she really knew all these people. Mattie was wearing a silky pink camisole, cutoff jeans, and Ugg boots. She looked pretty darn cold, but she didn't seem to notice. She was laughing in a braying-donkey kind of way, and strutting around like a wild turkey. I think she'd been drinking, smoking or snorting something more than beer. I saw her kissing one guy and then another. I decided to start counting. It's not that she was being all that obvious. But I could see her even when she stepped into the dark hallway, or cuddled up with someone in the shadowy corner on the couch in the living room. I counted seven guys and two women--and I only counted the ones where I saw tongue. If she gave somebody a little peck I didn't count it. I had promised myself that when she got to twelve I would leave, but it was taking longer than I thought it would. She was staggering and slurring her words, obviously slowing down. I stood up and was collecting my backpack and sweater, and that was that. I'd barely exchanged three words with anyone at the party. I was just watching, and that was entertainment enough for me. That's when Ty came up to me. "You're not leaving, are you?" he asked me.

I smiled and nodded. I mean what was I going say? I didn't want to blurt out that I'd been counting how many guys and gals Mattie had Frenched in the last 75 minutes, and I was disappointed she hadn't met the goal I'd set for her. That felt a little crass. So I stood there smiling stupidly for a few minutes, eyeing the crowd and wondering how I was going to squeeze out the front door that was crowded with incoming bodies, each holding a large empty plastic cup that wanted filling.

"Let me give you a ride," Ty said.

I tried to protest, I tried to tell him the bus stop was only a block away, but he got all Sir Galahad on me, saying I shouldn't be walking these streets alone, it wasn't safe and all. There was a part of me that wanted to say, "Hey, Ty--*you* shouldn't be walking the streets alone, but I have super powers and magic protection! No harm will befall me! I am good, bro!" But instead, as he was talking, I was noticing that he had turquoise colored eyes and these sweet dimples in the hollow of his cheeks. I haven't really felt all that attracted to anybody in a long while, so I thought, why not? Maybe we'll have a really good conversation on the way home and something will develop.

He had one of those little Toyota trucks with a bench seat across the front. I know guys say they like those trucks because they come in handy to help friends move furniture and lawn mowers and stuff like that. The gas mileage is much better than a full-sized truck. Not to mention they cost so much less. But hey, let's face it. They got the bench seat, rather than the buckets. So easy, so easy.

And that's pretty much what happened. He drove me part way home and then he stopped in a cul-de-sac, under a shady tree, where he thought it was truly dark, and I'm sure it looked dark to him, but of course to me, it was all very bright and shiny. He was damp with sweat since we'd just come from a crowded party, and his striped shirt was a little smelly, and his dark hair looked oily, and he had a zit starting on his chin, only a little red mark, not much, but c'mon, not very attractive. When he started to slide toward me I had a split second when I wanted to open the door and jump out. I could have done it too, because there was a bus stop right there on the corner, and I could easily read the fine print on the sign. I knew this bus line would take me to the light rail station. But I didn't do that. I let him kiss me, and then I let him French me, and Jesus Christ! He could do some things with his tongue that made me melt all the way from my throat to my crotch. His hands were awfully fast. He was working me over, just on top of my clothes, mind you, and still I was gasping for breath. He got to my belt buckle and I sat up and told him to stop. I don't know. I had to see this guy in class day after tomorrow, and I didn't want to give away the farm when all we'd ever done was exchange a few pleasantries. It's not like I expected him to eat a pizza and watch a Kings game with my family first, but I felt I deserved a little more attention than this. And so did he! Why don't men see it that way?

After I told him to stop, he drove me straight home without another word. He didn't say much more than a quick hello in class after that either. I'm writing a three next to his name in my notebook, because all he is to me now is one tongue and two hands, and that's it. I don't know that this boy even has a soul.

Chapter Eleven
Mariah's Journal

I've been so busy with my anthropological research that I pretty much neglected this notebook. I was just looking back at what I wrote about Ty, and I'm thinking I was a little hard on him. Sure, he shouldn't have tried to screw me like that in the truck, but he's no different than all the other guys, and a lot of the girls too. The week after my tongue and finger adventure with Ty I was at a dance club with some friends from my Greek philosophy class and I was watching them hook up with guys for a little tongue and finger action right on the dance floor. The E-ticket Ty-ride got me wondering. I hadn't realized there could be so much variation in a kiss. It's not like I wanted to be Mattie, but maybe I've been a good girl for too long. This particular night I wasn't drinking anything stronger than wine coolers, so I thought I could handle a little exploration. I set a limit of three--three guys and three wine coolers. I met Brad, Jake and Donavon that first night. I assigned them ones and twos in my notebook since I either let them tongue me or feel me up, but not both. I liked Donavon best, both for looks and for kissing. But he didn't ask me for my phone number or my last name. I was going to ask him for his email address, but he said he was going to the men's room and he didn't come back. Probably just as well, I thought.

I went out with these girls again to a different dance club a few days later. Again I set my limit at three drinks and three guys. I met Lionel, Joey, and Daniel. They were all disappointing. Lionel, one. Joey, two, and Daniel, three. I shouldn't have let Daniel have a three, but, well, I thought if I gave him a little more to work with he'd rise to the occasion so to speak. Nope, pretty dull. Maybe it was me. Maybe I'd already become jaded.

I figured I could pull Donavan's trick. I slipped away from him, saying I was going to the restroom, fully intending to leave the place. But then in a darkened corner of the bar I caught sight of Donavan. He saw me too, and the next thing I knew I was leaving with him. He lived in an apartment only two blocks away in a building upstairs from an art gallery. He didn't turn on too many lights, and I could see why--because I could see everything, of course, but he didn't know that. He was quite the slob, but his lips and tongue were magic. His bed sheets looked rumpled like he'd just slept with someone else on them, so I made him do it with me on this big suede couch, that looked and felt amazing. It was warm and plush, with a velvety nap like corduroy. I loved feeling my bare bottom on that soft surface. Donavan was great, the hands the tongue my eyes my ears my nipples. And his fingers, suddenly fingers drumming and gently twisting and massaging, like nothing I'd ever experienced. But then when it came to the act itself (and of course I insisted on protection, one I'd brought myself) it was back to the plain old traditional missionary position that Todd had to do every damn time. I thought, well, it is only the first time we've ever done it, maybe he's wanting to start slow. So after a little while when he expressed interest, I let him do it again. Same thing. Then he says to me that he needs to get up early in the morning, and "Do you need a ride home, sugar, or can you take care of yourself?" Jeez! I couldn't believe it, but truth be told I was relieved. I didn't want to stick around to give him a third ride in the morning. I thanked him for his interest in what I had to offer, and then I waddled down the stairs, feeling a little sorer, but a little wiser.

On the ground floor I took the time to peer into the enormous plate glass storefront window of the art gallery. A pack of large metallic dogs was spread across the floor of the main room. Any visitor would have to wade through these threatening looking statues, twelve or fourteen of them, all with their bronze lips curled back to reveal sharp, jagged silver-plated teeth. It was a startling display, but I didn't feel so very surprised. I mean if you're going to wander through junkyards, you've got to expect a few dogs will snap at your heels.

Chapter Twelve
Mariah's Journal

Five days ago I met Lucius, and tonight, at this very moment in fact, I am in his bed!

I know, I know, I had promised myself to retreat back into the safer, more objective status of observer, watcher on the side lines, professional grade pseudo anthropologist, no more cavorting with the natives for me. But this is different. This is romantic.

I'd gotten tired of the parties, the bars, the dance clubs. Craig told me to go about my business, live my life as I normally would. Instead I've been roaming the streets like a party animal. That's not me! I asked myself, what would I normally do if night were still night for me? The truth is most evenings I'd just stay home. Well, I wasn't ready to give up my questing yet, but I did want to tone it down. I found this sweet little coffee and dessert place on 21st a few block south of Zelda's. It used to be a fire house decades ago, and now someone has made it into a mellow little spot that smells of fresh roasted coffee beans and sugar cookies. They've got a black berry tart in a flaky dough served warm with melting vanilla ice cream on top. When I sit there in this big wooden rocker in the corner eating berries a la mode, I am content. Okay, I think, finally I have arrived; I will want for nothing more ever again. And that first night, that was true, I sat there, speaking to no one, wanting nothing but the quiet and the sweet dessert. I decided I could come here every night for the rest of my life, and if I didn't ever discover why I have this strange gift to see in the dark, that would be okay too. I felt redeemed.

The second night I met Lucius.

I arrived and was surprised to see the place was more crowded than the previous night, and the reason was Lucius. Lucius was sitting in a folding chair on a raised platform in the far corner playing Bach on an acoustic guitar. It was breathtaking to listen to, and watching his finger work was even better. I was smitten immediately.

I found an empty seat in the middle of the room. For most people, the live performance seemed to be background music. They were going about their business, chatting, eating and drinking, clacking spoons on saucers and forks on plates. I sat there and openly gawked. I couldn't help it.

Lucius had ash blonde hair, blue eyes, and a stubby little nose on his long angular face. He was dressed in denim and suede. A waitress came by so I was compelled to order. No dessert for me right now, I decided, I wanted my senses free of distraction, so I could focus on the music. I ordered red zinger tea.

There's not much more to tell. He spotted me in the crowd and I guess he could tell by the way my tongue was lolling that I was his number one fan. No, seriously I wasn't that bad. But he caught my eye, and we exchanged a few smiles and winks while he was playing. He came over and sat with me at a break, and we bonded over bowls of chocolate mousse. He was funny and smart and could quote e.e. cummings.

He said he knew this fun dance club that stayed open after hours, if I wanted to go with him when he finished at eleven. Of course I wanted to go with him. But I decided to play it cool. Not just for appearance's sake, but to test him, and to test myself. Would he be worth waiting for? I'd have to wait and see.

I came to the coffee house again the next night. A woman was playing flute. I was disappointed, but the music was lovely, a kind of Andean pan pipe sound. I settled in with my tea and my short bread and started reading King Lear.

Lucius bounded over to my table about 40 minutes later. "I hoped you'd be here again tonight," he said, and my heart melted. We talked and laughed for an hour or more. Again he asked me to the dance club, but again I said no. I had a midterm the next day. This time I would have my priorities straight.

The following night I was eating German chocolate cake, celebrating the fact that I'd aced the midterm. When Lucius arrived and asked me to the dance club, I thought okay. I can do this tonight.

We went outside and he led me to his car. The guy drives a beamer, two seater convertible, candy apple red! Suddenly it dawned on me that he was more than an itinerant musician. "What did you say you do for a living?" I asked.

"I'm in business," he said as he over-solicitously helped me buckle my seat belt.

"But what kind---?"

"I'm an associate executive at Ghost Owl Industries."

"Ghost Owl?" I repeated as he sped around a corner. This was synchronous; perhaps a marker to indicate that I was following the right path?

"We're quite a diverse company," he rattled off as if giving a presentation to the Rotary Club. "Our primary mission is the facilitation of interstate commerce and international export of Californian agricultural products. But my main duties have to do with the lobbying arm of the firm."

I have to admit I was quite impressed. "So you work down at the Capitol, talking to legislators about different bills and such?"

"Uh huh." He shifted into third gear and took the opportunity to squeeze my knee. I have to admit I didn't mind.

"But whose side are you on?" I asked mischievously. "What are you lobbying for?"

"Well, as I said, we're concerned primarily with the facilitation of--"

"Yeah, I know. Agriculture, right?"

"Exactly," he said with a grin. "I'm lobbying for farmers. Nobody can object to farmers, right? They're growing our food, our tomatoes and oranges and peaches and kiwis. And rice, can't forget California brown rice. Everybody love farmers, right?"

For the first time, I felt a little suspicious. Can anybody really trust a lobbyist? I wondered. They're like hired guns, they'll take up any cause for a price. But I decided for one night not to care. After all, we were just getting to know each other. We were just going to dance.

"The farmer in the dell!" he exclaimed suddenly. "Can't get more American than that, now can ya?" I laughed and said nothing.

He parked the car in a high-rise lot where we could see the white wedding cake Capitol building holding its own against the boxy high rises that are sprouting like weeds up and down J and K and L Streets. He draped his arms around me and we leaned against his car to look out at the city's skyline. I sighed, feeling contented. Maybe this was going to be a good fit, I thought. For some unknown reason I felt I could be at ease with Lucius; I could relax. I'd spent the last four weeks rushing around at night like a raccoon, creeping into dark places and peering into shadowed corners. Lifting up a lot of rocks. I'd forgotten to appreciate this gift, to take the time to look out and see how beautiful were the new sights my eyes were displaying for me.

I could see everything, and it was astounding. Of course it wasn't the typical city by night everyone else was seeing; it was something completely different. Everywhere there were jewels, green and blue and black. The buildings were made of colored sand and gemstones, the sky was shimmering with pearls, the entire landscape appeared to be under a liquid sheen, waving like the water in a florescent aquarium. The Capitol, the beautiful capitol of my home town, it appeared as if it were made of white sugar, shimmering so bright it almost hurt my eyes to look at it.

We took an elevator to the ground floor and we strode a couple blocks to an alley behind a hotel. I knew it was dark down there, but I could see it all so I wasn't afraid. Logical-thinking Mariah gave a little tug to the reasoning side of my brain, warning me that a young naive college girl should think twice before heading off into a dark alley with a man she's only known a few days. But my gut told me to trust, so I did. Lucius took my hand, thinking he'd need to lead me in the dark, but of course I could see better than he could.

The alley was well-maintained, cleanly swept, and dead-ended in a row of four long dumpsters. It was a little stinky, but not over-powering. Two of the dumpsters were a dull olive green, presumably for garbage, and the others were cornflower blue, for recycling. There were five doors, three on the north building and two on the south. The north building looked closed for the night, but lights were on in the ground floor of the south building. The first door we passed was ajar and a tall skinny man in jeans and a sweat shirt stood smoking in the door way. Lucius nodded to him, and the guy snuffed out his cigarette and ducked back inside. Lucius led me to the second door. It was painted forest green against the red brick. It reminded me of Christmas, it seemed so cheery. It felt like a treat to come to this secret place; I was happy and excited. I spun around like a kid, just having fun.

Then I caught sight of a man crouched in the corner of the alley. He had a neatly trimmed beard and high sculpted cheekbones. I had seen this same man a month ago camped on the front steps of St. Francis of Assisi church. He looked at me with frantic eyes, and at first I thought he was scared because he had been discovered hiding back here in the alley. I spread my hands to indicate I meant him no harm, but he shook his head. "Do not," he said softly in an accented voice. "Do not eat or drink anything while you're in this place."

I looked at him and then at Lucius, surprised and confused that my date had not heard the insistent warning of this strange man near the dumpsters. Lucius was knocking again, and the door was swinging out. We stepped back and I turned to look again at the man behind me. "Listen to me!" the man hissed in a voice as loud as he dared. "Listen to me!"

I nodded, then followed Lucius inside.

The room was deliberately dark and mysterious, though of course I could see that it was cheap looking plywood dividers covered with thin and ragged curtains, black or navy blue. The space was cut into narrow passageways, so I obediently followed Lucius as he led me toward the sound of loud music. Finally we emerged in a large open space with a high ceiling. A bar dominated the center of the room and what looked like a mezzanine looked down at us. I imagined that if one's eyes saw darkness, the room might look plush and romantic, but to me, it looked garish and artificial. The walls were painted with mottled white and gray to simulate marble, I suppose. There was metallic looking grill work here and there. I guess it was supposed to resemble wrought iron, but to my eyes it appeared to be chicken wire or maybe even some kind of foil. A live band with a full brass section and electric guitars played jazz against one wall. Now they were hot. They were worth the price of enduring this strange space, I decided as Lucius led me to the dance floor.

He held me tight and then twirled me away, and I could see him glancing up. I looked up too, and was surprised to see a half dozen or more men, most middle aged or older in expensive business suits, crowding around the cheap chicken wire balcony above, to glare down at the dancers below. On occasion one would glance away and beckon to someone or other with a finger snap or gesture. A waiter in tight pants and vest would appear with a tray or a drink, and I even saw one man point down at a tall buxom girl dancing to my left. Lucius caught me gaping, and touched my cheek in what seemed to be a gesture of affection, but I saw him glancing upward again too. He squinted and grimaced, looking confused or concerned, I really couldn't tell. He grabbed me suddenly and pulled me close. "Let me get you a drink," he said, more command than offer. "What do you want?"

I remembered the urgent plea of the man in the alley, and I wasn't all that thirsty anyway. "I'm good," I murmured demurely.

"Oh, you've got to drink something," he insisted. "Let me order for you. I bet I know what a girl like you would like. I've seen you've got quite the sweet tooth. Have you ever had a Brandy Alexander?"

I smiled, tempted, but my gut told me to heed the warning. "I want to dance," I told him, as I dug my fingers into his hair. "Let's just dance."

He smiled at me, nonplussed, then looked up again. There was a dark haired heavily-jowled man above us in a double-breasted suit. Lucius appeared to give him a clipped nod and shrug. The man strode away.

"Who was that?" I asked. Lucius looked down at me startled. "What?" he said abruptly. "What are you looking at?"

"There are a lot of people upstairs," I said. "Is that someone you know up there?"

"A lot of people I know come here," he told me in a harsh decisive voice. "Don't worry about it. It's like I said, I work down here."

I grinned at him as we swayed to the music. "They don't

look like no farmers up there," I said flirtatiously. He looked up again, obviously surprised that I could see everyone clearly up there. But then he had to laugh. "Not your typical farmer anyway," he confirmed. Then he kissed me! Oh, God, all my resolutions about taking it slow went right out the window. And then I came here with him to his apartment.

I guess I should say right now that Lucius is at least ten years older than I am. I feel lucky to have such a great rapport with a man who can teach me so much, and well, I've learned a lot just in the past hour. Light years beyond Todd, Ty or Donavon.

Lucius is asleep now. I pulled my notebook out of my backpack and started writing, because I don't need to turn on a light.

Chapter Thirteen
Rafa

The notebook ended. Rafa pushed his hair away from his face and crushed his empty cardboard espresso cup. This didn't sound good. Mariah was so damn naive! Didn't she see that those men upstairs were all shopping for ass when they were staring at the girls below? She got away that night, but did she go back there with this Lucius? Who the hell was he anyway? A lobbyist? More like a pimp maybe. And why the hell hadn't she dated any of these journal entries? She could have written this weeks ago or last night. There was no way of knowing.

He stood up, searching for his cell phone. He had to call Dale. But wait--maybe there was another notebook. Phone in his hand he headed back into Mariah's bedroom to look.

Chapter Fourteen
Dale

Dale woke up to find himself wrapped around Luisa, his fiancée. He glanced over her shoulder at the alarm clock. 5:55. For some reason, the repeating numbers made him think of his father, the late Charlie Easter. Charlie would have come up with a story to explain the significance of the sudden emphasis that the universe was placing on the number five. Or maybe that the universe wanted Dale to notice the number 5. Maybe it was a clue, some kind of a sign. Charlie would have been out of bed by now, looking through his wife's collection of books on metaphysical themes, seeking a tome on numerology. Dale looked again at the clock. 5:57. Okay, he could ignore a number like that. See, Dad, he said in his head to the invisible Charlie that resided there, if you just wait a minute, the urge to rush off on a wild goose chase will go away.

It wasn't that Dale didn't have a spiritual side. He just hadn't immersed himself in the spiritual quest the way his father had done. Dale himself wasn't sure if he had an atheist streak or if his aversion to all things metaphysical was an act of rebellion against Charlie Easter's mad dash after the ever-changing path of universal energy. But Dale had tended to follow his mother's more grounded view of reality. At least he did until his mother, Geneva, a superior court judge, had retired and returned to her Native American roots in Arizona where she too could pursue her particular brand of spirit worship. Dale had been nonplussed by that.

God herself finally came calling on Dale when he felt drawn to, and then fell in love with, a wise and beautiful woman who happened to have a severe form of Asperger's Syndrome. Luisa Villasenor could only communicate by typing on an alternative communication device. She had two or three machines, but she generally preferred to use a simple iPad. She had one with a robotic voice, but Luisa most often preferred that her companions just read her words off the screen themselves. If she was speaking before a crowd, she often hired a young woman to read the words she typed aloud to the audience. She and Dale also had a system of sign language they'd developed together to communicate. Still sign language could present a special challenge since Luisa didn't always have complete control over her motor movements. She was subject to uncontrollable repetitive movements like rocking and hand-flapping. Both she and those around her at times found this frustrating, but most often she and Dale had learned to work around it all.

Dale's thoughts immediately turned to his missing half-sister, Mariah, who had been out of touch with her family for four days now. He pulled away from Luisa to roll onto his back and stare at the ceiling. The room was dim, and he wondered if it was too early to call Rafa, Mariah's flat mate--who happened to be Luisa's brother. That's the kind of thing Charlie would have loved--the synchronicity of the two family's connections. Anyway, Dale knew Rafa felt somehow responsible, as if he should have kept a closer watch on Mariah. That wasn't Rafa's job. Dale himself had led a pretty free-wheeling life when he got into college. He knew what it was like.

Luisa squeaked and rolled over to rest her head on his chest. "Sorry, Lu," he murmured. "I didn't mean to wake you."

She began to make a low undulating sound in the back of her throat, and she clenched Dale's T shirt, wadding it up in her fist. Dale knew this as a signal for help, and he began to slowly but firmly stroke her head. Luisa calmed and breathed deeply. Dale closed his eyes. He knew Luisa was worried about Mariah too.

His relationship with Luisa had begun as internet chats. Though most others were astonished by Luisa's intelligence, her knowledge of world religions, her spiritual depth, Dale had been attracted by her clever wit, her sense of humor and her compassion.

Dale's stepmother, Samantha, had known Luisa as a child and teen, and she warned Dale that life would not be easy if he chose to pursue a romantic relationship with her. Dale was the first to admit that Samantha had been right, but no matter, life with Luisa was worth it. Luisa could shower, dress and groom herself independently, though she sometimes needed help with buttons, zippers and shoelaces. She could use the microwave and assist with the cleaning and cooking, but generally she needed help to get going. Helping Luisa with stuff like this was not an issue for Dale. That he could handle. But when they went out in public together, people immediately assumed that he was her hired caretaker, rather than her lover. Couldn't they see how gentle and beautiful she was? She had thick black hair and her expressive eyes were a stunning shade of amber green. How could anyone fail to notice how desirable she was? Certainly any man would fall in love with her. If they didn't, they just weren't paying attention.

When they first met, Dale and Luisa went out often with family members, giving their courtship a nineteenth century feeling. Dale felt Luisa's mother Anna was overprotective of her daughter, but then he noticed his step-mother was also hovering near him. "Do you see?" Samantha would whisper. "Luisa is mesmerized by the ceiling fans in here. Anna touches her cheek and that helps her re-focus. Now she can read the menu. This is probably a routine they've worked out." Dale realized he was being tutored and he paid close attention.

Most often Luisa moved quickly and naturally in public. But occasionally something might disturb her—a loud noise, bright lights, a tight crowd, shifts in temperature. She might begin to rock, squeal, even dart across a room. Dale watched the ways Anna and Rafa supported Luisa with firm touch and soft words. He was eager to take Luisa on a real date, just the two of them.

When Luisa came to California, Dale took her to one of his favorite restaurants, a bistro that specialized in Italian-Mexican fusion, famous for its meatball and spinach salad. They arrived early in the evening to beat the crowds. Luisa seemed unusually manic. She darted away from Dale, past the hostess, pausing to giggle and sway beneath a ceiling fresco of blue sky and doves.

"Sorry," Dale said to the hostess as he trailed after Luisa. He squeezed Luisa shoulder in a firm grip as she had told him to do. "Shall we sit here?" he asked the hostess gamely, indicating the closest table. The confused-looking hostess meekly agreed.

Feeling a bit apprehensive, Dale moved his chair close to Luisa's so he could grab her if needed. His mind drifted to Samantha's stories of taking her students on "community-based instruction," remembering how a girl with Down Syndrome had once grabbed a Chicken McNugget from a stranger's plate. He sipped his water and for the first time wondered if he could really handle a relationship with this woman.

Luisa appeared to be skimming the menu. She whipped her iPad from her bag. "I want meatball salad," she typed rapidly.

"The meatball salad is legendary here," Dale said softly. "But did you see the shrimp enchiladas? You can order anything you want."

"Yes," she typed. "And Oaxacan fish stew sounds good too. I'll have them another time. Tonight I want salad."

Oaxacan—what? Dale glanced down at the menu. This must be a new item. "Are you going to have mole sauce?" Luisa typed. "You told me that's your favorite. They have it on four dishes."

Dale's mouth dropped open. She had read the entire six-page menu in less than three minutes. "Can we have the calamari appetizer?" she typed.

He nodded slowly, finding it hard to keep up. "Sure."

A waiter appeared. Before he could speak, Luisa lifted the menu. With broad gestures and squeaky vocalizations, she pointed to her selection.

The waiter seemed unsurprised. "Meatball and spinach salad," he noted. "Good choice. And for you, sir?" Dale placed his order. "Anything to drink?" The waiter prompted and again Luisa was squeaking in staccato bursts, waving her fingers near her cheek in an approximation of the American Sign Language sign for wine.

Dale breathed deeply, seeing that the waiter was stiffening, his jaw set. Dale cleared his throat. "Chardonnay or Merlot?" he asked Luisa, already familiar with her preferences.

She signed white and Dale ordered the Chardonnay. "Nothing but water for me," he said feeling it would be wise to keep his mind clear.

The dining room was beginning to fill up as the waiter headed to the bar. Dale exhaled, beginning to relax. But Luisa was thrusting her iPad toward him. "I take pics," she typed, then started a slide show of photos she had taken with Mariah and Rafa that afternoon while Dale was at work. The sentences she was typing were fragmented and clipped. This was not unusual: though Luisa was capable of writing academic-quality prose as well as thoughtful and leisurely dialogue, she also was practiced at writing abbreviated sentences to get her thoughts out rapidly. But now she seemed agitated and Dale worried that she was nervous being alone with him. She began to rock and moan, emitting a low guttural hum from the back of her throat. Again he gripped her shoulder and firmly rubbed her back. "Are you nervous?" he whispered.

She looked stricken as she signed NO. "You know I

vocalize like this sometimes," she typed over the photos.

"Oh, I know that; I understand," he assured her. "But the photos. You're moving through them awfully fast. We can look at them slowly. And we can talk slowly. Like we did when we were at your house in Connecticut."

She squealed loudly and began to laugh in a near-hysterical pitch. "Oh, Dale! You are right! I guess I am nervous."

People were staring as the hostess appeared at the table. "Is everything all right sir?" she asked pointedly.

"Yes, we're fine," Dale said curtly.

"We have tables open on the patio," the hostess said in a leading voice. "Perhaps you would prefer--"

"I said we were fine."

The hostess scurried away. Dale turned to Luisa. "Let's get out of here," he said.

Luisa flapped her hands rapidly but still managed to type. "I want my salad."

"No problem," he agreed. "We'll get it to go."

"No," she signed, yelling wordlessly now as every head turned in her direction. She grabbed Dale's hand, beginning again to type. "This is what it's like for me. You can't take it personally."

"I'm not taking it personally," he said, lowering his voice. "I'm insulted for you."

She began to rock in small circles. "Your feelings are YOUR feelings. They have nothing to do with me. YOU must learn to deal with them."

She glared at him even as she rocked, and he knew she was

right. He tightened his hold on her hand, and she smiled and giggled as if she were a little girl. He had to laugh too. Then he caught sight of an elderly man at the next table craning his neck to look at them, and he gave the man an angry leer. Luisa continued to smile and rock. "Let people stare," she typed to Dale. "They're going to learn something about romantic love." She pulled on his arm, until he leaned forward and kissed her gently on the mouth. "Listen to them gasp!" she typed quickly. "I think this is the most fun I've ever had in a restaurant!"

Their first year together, Luisa made Dale take her out often. One night she typed to him. "Dale, I think you are finally comfortable going out with me in public."

"What are you talking about?" he protested. "I've always felt comfortable--"

She interrupted him with her laughter. "If you are lying to save my feelings," she typed, "you know by now that isn't necessary. If you are lying to yourself, Dale, shame on you! You are better than that!"

He sunk onto the couch at her feet. "Okay, busted," he admitted. "I guess it was a little of both."

"You know I believe that life on the physical plane is an illusion. We are all playing roles as if we were in a movie or stage play. The part of a woman with an unusual disability is the one I've chosen to play this lifetime. I knew it would be hard, and I never thought I would be blessed enough to play the roles that come easily to other women. I wanted to go out and celebrate, I wanted to serve as an example to other people that other realities are possible. And I wanted you to let go of your fears of being judged, your fear of being seen as someone who is strange and different. I think I'd rather stay home with you more often now. I'd rather stay at home, order in a pizza and watch videos, rather than going out so often."

Dale waited patiently while she typed. When she handed him the iPad he was surprised and delighted. Of course he agreed.

Conversations were like this sometimes. She would type and pass him the iPad. He would read it, then type a response to her. It made their life together feel slow and leisurely. Perhaps this was the greatest gift of all, to get off the treadmill and realize how important it was to savor life. He had rebelled against his father's job-hopping life style and followed his mother into a life as a lawyer. He was a hard worker and had risen quickly in his law firm. He had achieved a seven-figure status. But after moving in with Luisa, he was willing to let that go. He found a job at an environmental firm where he worked no more than 30 hours a week, so he could spend more time with Luisa. "Who cares if people think you're my care giver?" Luisa had told him. "In many ways you are my care giver! There is no shame in that. I'm not embarrassed that I need that help, and I am proud that you are willing to give it to me."

Despite the cut in hours, he still made a very good living. Luisa's salary more than made up for the shortfall. Though she could have continued to telecommute and serve as a part time faculty member at Yale, she had accepted a full-time position at the Berkeley School of Theology when she moved west. She still taught only internet classes, but the college wanted her to hold a session or two in-person classes each semester, so professors and students could put names and faces together. Dale was happy to accompany her to her first week of in-person classes. He knew Luisa was a bit nervous since she had never done this before.

Luisa had already contacted the class, explaining her disability in her first online lecture, so the students seemed curious but not surprised as they watched her enter the room. She used a robotic voice for the first few minutes, then confessed to the class that she preferred to hear a human voice reading her words: would a woman or two volunteer to read her writing aloud as she typed? Two students agreed to take turns.

Dale was excited to see Luisa in action. He was looking forward to her lecture, which she had told him, was on the similarities and differences between Christianity and Islam. But then she sat down, urging the students to move to closer chairs, and typed that she hoped they would get to know each other better this day.

Dale sat apart from the others, since he was not a member of the class, but finally she pointed to him. "I want you to meet Dale. He is my care giver as well as my lover, and I am blessed to have him in my life."

There was a stunned silence as the young woman reading the words paused in surprise after reading the word "lover" aloud. "Oh," she murmured after finishing the sentence. There were a few whispers and titters of laugher. Dale felt his cheeks color, but he wasn't sure if it was because people were assessing him as a sexual partner for their teacher, or whether he was angry that the group was doing the same to Luisa. He felt an urge to stand up, but he had no idea what he would do or say. He knew, as Luisa had told him, that these feelings were his, and they had nothing to do with her. Still he wasn't sure what to do about that.

"I feel blessed," Luisa typed again, "that I can serve as a role model--not just for people with disabilities--but for anyone who wants to test the boundaries of possibility. Yes, I have a severe disability, but I am not unlike any other woman in my needs and desires."

There was a hush then, a fullness of energy in the room. Dale looked around and saw nearly every head nodding in understanding and compassion. I guess this is awe, he thought. At that moment a young woman with jet-black hair and heavy eyeliner broke the silence. "You go, girl!" she declared in a husky voice. The room exploded in laughter and then applause at the over-used cliché, but Luisa was squealing and laughing in delight. And then the most shocking thing of all: Dale began to cry. He couldn't remember the last time he had cried, maybe when Roy Henderson poked his fingers in Dale's left eye in seventh grade, maybe that was the last time. But these tears didn't flow out of pain, they manifested out of some bittersweet pining, some happy fulfillment, the witnessing of a miracle. Oh, so this was the miracle. Not that Luisa was smart when she appeared to be cognitively impaired, but that someone as cynical as Dale was could soften up and cry because he was so damn happy to be in love with her. Now that was a miracle if there ever was one. He quickly wiped his eyes, but it was too late. Luisa had seen, and she gave him a toothy grin. She had never looked happier.

"Daaaaya!" Dale jerked awake when he heard Luisa's labored pronunciation of his name. She stood at the side of the bed with a cup of hot water she'd heated in the microwave with a tea bag floating in it. In her other hand was the phone. "Aaafa!" she squealed and Dale sat up, knowing Rafa was on the phone.

Dale reached out to take the phone. "Dale," Rafa said immediately. "I've been up all night reading Mariah's journal." He paused and Dale was afraid he might be crying. "I'm really scared," Rafa concluded.

Chapter Fifteen
Dale

Dale pulled his SUV into a high-rise parking lot. Rafa sat beside him on the passenger side, Mariah's notebook in his lap. "Do you think this is the lot Mariah describes?" he asked Dale.

"I don't know," Dale said, "but one way or another, it's got to be close."

Dale pulled into a space near the 2nd floor elevator. "You've got to go park on the top," Rafa said insistently.

"What?" Dale asked, unsure if he'd heard Rafa correctly.

"You need to go to the top," Rafa said in a matter of fact way. "It's how Mariah describes it. They went to the top."

"What does it matter where I park?" Dale asked impatiently, his hand still on the ignition key, not sure if he should re-start the car or not.

Rafa looked away. He was breathing deeply and blinking rapidly. "I know it sounds silly, but you know, maybe if we follow her footsteps exactly, maybe--" He looked up quickly to glance at Dale then lowered his head again. "I just think it matters," he concluded, his voice catching. He stared down at his hands, and Dale could see he was batting his eyes to blink back tears.

Dale leaned over and put his arm around Rafa's shoulder. At that, Rafa surprised Dale, turning and giving him a full embrace. He began to weep openly in Dale's arms. Dale patted him on the back and waited patiently. A sudden amusing thought struck him, that here on a Sunday morning, in a deserted parking lot, two men embracing in a car, a passerby might think Dale was a homosexual predator, picking up on a younger man. Luisa will get a kick out that. In the past, Dale might have shirked away, embarrassed by Rafa's open neediness. Dale might have been worried about what other people would think. But not now. Now he welcomed the open affection of his family. He could celebrate it even when something as upsetting as Mariah's disappearance had prompted it. He rubbed Rafa's shoulder. "I love you, Rafa. We're going find her. It's going to be okay. We have to stay positive."

"Okay," Rafa agreed in a gravelly voice as he pulled back. "Thanks, man."

Dale nodded and turned the key in the ignition. They drove to the top of the parking structure.

Rafa got out and went to the edge of the rooftop to look out at the city. "This must be the place," he said. "Look," he pointed out toward Capitol Park. "It's just as she described it."

Rafa stood there looking out, breathing deeply, sinking into a tai chi stance, knees slightly bent, hips squared. Dale watched him, again feeling impatient. He thought of Luisa, and all she had taught him. Then he reminded himself that Rafa was Luisa's brother; that he had been raised in a household where conversation and movement were slow. He put his hand on Rafa's forearm, as Luisa often put her hand on Dale's arm. She needed Dale to help balance her. Maybe Rafa would help Dale slow down now. Help him find the right path, rather than rushing off. Rafa turned to Dale and smiled. "Ready?" Rafa asked and Dale nodded.

They headed down L Street and then back up J. They circled the blocks around the Hyatt, the Sheraton, and the Citizen. "Would have been easier if she'd written down the address," Dale mumbled.

"Hey, we're lucky she mentioned that it was by a hotel," Rafa countered.

"And we're lucky there aren't that many hotels around here."

Nothing they saw in the alleys between these downtown buildings fit the description in Mariah's journal. They hiked over to K Street and headed west toward the Holiday Inn. "I can't believe the police weren't interested in looking for this dive!" Rafa said.

"I think they still aren't sure that Mariah's really missing," Dale said. "I think they've seen too many cases where a girl her age shows up back in town after taking a ride to San Francisco or Tahoe with a new boyfriend or something."

Rafa was silent at that, and Dale listened to the sound of their footsteps hitting the pavement in rapid synch. "Rafa," he asked slowly. "Do you think that could be what's happened? Do you think she just took off without telling any of us? I mean is that even possible?"

"I don't know," Rafa said, staring down at the ground. "Maybe. I hope so."

They reached the Holiday Inn and jogged around it, but the building was set off in a plaza with no alleys nearby. Definitely not the place.

Dale looked at Rafa, who looked like he might cry again. "Did you get any sleep last night?" he asked.

"I think I dozed for an hour or so around four this morning."

"What about food?" Dale asked. "Have you eaten anything today?"

"Yeah, sure," Rafa said in an offhand way. "I'm fine."

"I think we should stop and get you a meal, and--"

"Dale," Rafa interrupted. "We've got one more hotel. Have

you forgotten? They've just re-opened the old Senator!"

Dale had forgotten. "The Senator! It's right across from Capitol Park. It's got to be the place."

They picked up their speed nearly running down the sparsely populated streets toward the stately old hotel. They slowed down when they reached it, circling it slowly, creeping into an alley on the west side, and then coming back around to check out an alley on the east side. "Dale!" Rafa exclaimed as they stood expectant at the opening to the dead ended passageway. "Look! It's just as she described it: neat and clean, well swept, dumpsters--and check it out--two doorways—yeah, this is the south building! Red brick and a green door." He grabbed Dale's arm and jumped up and down. "This is it!"

Dale nodded and pulled away from Rafa, his head lowered. He slid his left hand deep into his hip pocket and suddenly Dale realized that he was searching for a pack of cigarettes. Funny; he hadn't had that urge in nearly three years, not since right after his father died. He took a deep breath, but could barely exhale. He would do this without cigarettes, because he would not go down that road again. He strode forward, lifted his fist and pounded it on the green door. "Open up, you jackasses!" he yelled angrily. "Open this damn door!" He kicked the door a couple times for good measure, but there was neither a sound nor any movement at the windows. "I'll kick this blasted door in if I have to," Dale hollered.

He felt Rafa's hand on his back. "Dale, man! You can't kick the door in, because Mariah said the door opens out. So that won't work."

Dale leaned back against Rafa. "I guess that was pretty silly looking," he said, adding a self-deprecating snort.

"No problem," Rafa said. "Give me a minute and I'll start crying again." They both laughed.

"Hey, look," Rafa said, suddenly sprinting down to the end of the alley. "It's a sleeping bag--hidden here by this dumpster! Maybe that man Mariah saw in the alley--maybe he's still living down here." Rafa shrugged. "He's got to come back sometime. Maybe he knows something."

Dale nodded and pulled his cell phone from his pocket. "I think it's time to give the police another call."

Chapter Sixteen
Mariah's Journal

After my magical night with Lucius, he treated me to breakfast at the Fox and Goose and then he even drove me to school. I thought I'd died and gone to heaven. I could get used to service like that, I thought.

We'd exchanged cell numbers, but I didn't hear from him all day. I'm not so old fashioned that I expect a bouquet of flowers after a night of love-making, but I thought he'd at least text me. After my afternoon nutrition class, I decided to send him a text, asking if he'd be playing guitar at the coffee house that night. He didn't respond. I'm not going to lie, I felt pretty bad about that. I tried to remind myself that he was older than me and had a pretty important job. Maybe he was in meetings or something like that.

As I walked to the light rail station, I wondered if maybe I should skip the coffee house that night. After all, it could be awkward to run into him there if he was no longer interested. Omygod! So silly, I told myself. I have the right to go wherever I want to go. If he feels awkward, let him stay away from the coffee house. I was determined to not let it bother me.

I didn't hear from him that night, and I didn't see him at the coffee house either. That was fine. I was due for an early night and hopefully an evening with Rafa. I hoped he would be home, and he was.

He was slouched on the couch, his feet on our third hand coffee table. He was watching the latest Hobbit movie on the DVD player. I slumped down beside him on the couch and he paused his movie. "No Angie tonight?" I asked.

He gave me a funny look. "I broke up with Angie almost two weeks ago," he said. "How come you don't know that?"

His voice had an accusatory tone to it. I knew immediately what he was implying. I'd been out so much this past month that we barely have had time to talk anymore. I felt bad, and yet all I could murmur was, "I don't know, Rafa. I don't know."

"You haven't been home much lately," he said, and this time there was no rancor or accusation. It was a plain fact. And yet, now I felt defensive, now I felt a little spark of annoyance.

"You're out all the time with different women," I countered. "One girl after the other, so many I can barely keep track of them! And yet you're going to get all pissy if I do the same?"

His head reared back. "Is that what you're doing?" he asked, seeming to be sincerely interested, curious. "You've been going out with one guy after the other?"

"No!" I protested, again on the defensive. I paused, knowing that was exactly what I'd been doing, only I hadn't been lucky enough to meet a guy like Rafa who would invite me over to meet his roommate and his friends, and cook a meal for me, and show me off. Even if Rafa was moving through these women kind of quick, at least he was treating them right while he was with them. At least, it looked that way to me. I guess where Rafa's concerned, I am rather biased.

Maybe I should have said all these things I was thinking to Rafa. Maybe I should have told him about Lucius, and how I was feeling disappointed and sad because apparently I was no more than a one-night stand to him. Maybe I should have told Rafa about my gift and about how it compelled me to go out into the night to observe and explore. But at that moment I suddenly felt tired. "Can I watch the rest of your movie with you?" I asked.

He smiled, also looking tired and sympathetic. "Sure," he said, and he lifted his arm to drape it around me. I rested my head on his shoulder and we sat together like that and watched the movie.

Chapter Seventeen
Mariah's Journal

I'm sitting in the cafeteria at Mercy General Hospital. It's 1:30 in the morning. The police came into the emergency room a half hour ago. They'd gotten my backpack out of that club, so they brought it here, trying to find out who it belonged to. That sweet Sister Gabriel brought it over to me. She's been so nice, that I felt a little bad sneaking away, but really, there's no need for me to hang around. I'm okay now. I was feeling kind of empty, and I decided a hamburger and a cup of soft serve ice cream would go a long way toward easing that ache.

I had started the evening at the coffee house, nibbling on a sugar cookie and outlining my term paper for my Renaissance art history class. I was feeling peaceful again. Lucius was way back in the rearview mirror; I swear I wasn't even thinking about him.

Suddenly I heard the wrought iron chair legs scraping against the concrete floor. I looked up to see him seating himself across from me at the table. "Hey, girl," he said, and I felt my stomach jump into my throat. He is awfully good looking, with a wicked little uncertain smile, and his voice has a husky quality to it. I found myself smiling at him. Smiling! Involuntarily charmed! It was disgusting. All the time, my lips are smiling, my breasts and groin are tingling, and yet I'm hearing him say "Hey, girl," in that sexy voice, and I'm wondering if he's forgotten my name.

I stared at him so befuddled that I couldn't even form my mouth to offer a greeting. "Hey, boy. Little man-child that you are. Insincere spoiled brat!" That's what I should have said. But no, I sat there, unable to think, a prisoner of my hormones, just throbbing, infatuation personified.

He was undeterred by my silence. "How've you been?" he said casually, reaching for my hand, and I let him take it for crying out loud, I let him have my hand. I let him have my eyes, I dropped them into the blue pool that is his eyes, I gave them away. "Let's go dancing," he said decisively.

Finally I found my voice. I pulled my hand back to my notebook. "I didn't really like that dance club of yours," I said. "I think I'll pass."

"Sweetheart, everybody likes that club! It's exclusive and it's hot! You didn't give it much of chance. We didn't even order anything to eat. They serve an amazing filet mignon, grilled salmon if you prefer fish."

I licked my lips. "I've already eaten dinner," I said. "But thank you for the invitation. I need to get on with my classwork."

He reached forward abruptly and grabbed my hand again. "Mariah," he said firmly, "I really want you to give me another chance."

My mouth dropped open and I stared at his beautiful face. Yes, of course I'll give you another chance: I wanted to say that, and yet my mouth wasn't working. Yes, of course, but please let's stay here at this sweet and peaceful coffee house. Let's go to my apartment and you can meet Rafa. Let's go to my mother's house and you can meet her. Let's go to a movie or an art gallery. But instead I was silent, inexplicably silent, as if I was compelled by an unknowable force to agree to his terms. "Okay," I said, surprised at my own acquiescence, embarrassed that I was smiling again, girlishly grasping his hand tighter, and standing to go with him. Was I hoping that he was going to be the man I wanted him to be, or was I just playing along? I don't even know now.

We drove downtown and he parked his car. I got out of the car, strapping on my backpack to bring with me. "You can leave that in the car," he said.

"No," I said, surprised again at my own insistence. "I want to bring it with me."

"You won't need it," he said, smirking as if I were a child who needs instruction.

Then something funny happened. I gave him a look, I think it was what my mother called her "teacher look," an unwavering glare is what it is, a nonverbal message that I have made a decision and you will comply or get out of my way. And he did. "Bring it if you want," he said breezily. "Whatever rows your boat."

I was feeling very confused by now. I didn't know why I needed to bring my backpack, and what's more, I didn't know why I was coming here to the dance club with Lucius to begin with. And yet I continued into the elevator and down the multicolored downtown block at his side, striding past glittering store windows and florescent yellow lights.

We entered the alleyway, and the green door seemed to shine like an emerald. It was beckoning me. There was something inside that I needed to see, I was sure of it. I stepped back, a bit startled by this revelation, and I stared at Lucius in surprise. This had nothing to do with him, I was sure of that. How satisfying it would be, I thought, to turn to him right now, and say, *You can go now. I'll handle it from here on in.* I almost laughed out loud at the thought. Lucius looked at me strangely. He seemed to have noticed this inexplicable change in me too. "You okay?" he asked.

"Great," I responded, and my voice sounded loud and commanding.

He knocked on the door and we went inside. The place was cheap and mundane, nothing mysterious here. And yet I approached with an overwhelming curiosity: what would I find here? Something amazing, something amazing was going to happen. I walked quickly, eagerly.

Lucius steered me to a table. "Let's have a drink first," he said. He held out a chair for me, and gently grasped the straps of my backpack as if he were helping me take off my coat. I didn't want to let go of it, but it seemed silly not to. Certainly I wasn't going to dance with a heavy back pack strapped to my shoulders. I sat down and shoved my backpack under the table at my feet.

"Let me order for you," he said, and raised his hand to summon a waiter. "Have you ever had an Appletini or a Long Island Iced Tea?"

The waiter appeared, dish cloth draped formally across his forearm. I leaned past Lucius toward the waiter. "I'll have a martini," I said. "A regular gin martini."

Lucius reared back in surprise at my decisiveness. "I'll have the same," he told the man, "but make mine with a splash of cranberry juice."

Cranberry juice, I thought. That'll make it bitter--to fit your personality! I myself was sticking with Paul Newman's instruction to Robert Redford in *The Sting:* always drink gin with a mark; he can't tell if you cut it. I was looking around for a place to dump this little drink because I was more certain than ever that I shouldn't eat or drink anything in here. I couldn't imagine why I wasn't supposed to eat anything, but it seemed obvious that I should stay sober and keep my wits about me.

The waiter brought our drinks. Mine had a big and luscious stuffed green olive soaking in the gin. I was tempted, but still, didn't dare. "Mmmm," Lucius murmured as I fingered the spear that held the olive, removing it from the drink. "Nothing tastier than a gin-soaked olive."

"Oh," I said quickly, "then please have mine. I don't like olives."

Lucius looked annoyed that I was once again declining

food. "You don't like olives? I can't believe that. Would you rather have an onion or a lemon twist? Name it and I'll go get it for you."

I gave him a toothy contrived grin. "Mmmm--maraschino cherries please! And bring a lot of them."

Lucius exhaled through his nose, and I have to admit I felt pleased that he was so annoyed. He gave a quick nod of his head. "Be right back."

As soon as he left, I grabbed the lovely funneled glass and was surprised to discover it was made of plastic. Jeez, this was a cheap joint. No matter. Lifting my backpack so it wouldn't get wet, I began to sprinkle my cocktail across the shag rug under the table. It wasn't the best choice since the rug--like everything else in the place--was pretty darn cheap. The drink didn't so much soak into the pile as pool there. Still I managed to dispose of the whole thing. There was no dry spot left for my backpack so I stood up and put it on my chair. Lucius was approaching. I picked up the speared olive tilting on the table and I stepped forward to greet him.

"Here baby," I said, thrusting the olive toward his lips, "here's that luscious treat for you."

He jerked his head away as if threatened by this tiny morsel of food. That's when the bells began to ring in my head. How stupid I'd been! I stepped back.

"What's the matter with you?" he blurted at me, grabbing the olive and tossing it unceremoniously onto the shiny white table cloth.

I stood frozen for a moment, mesmerized by the crystal-clear water glass filled with cherries that he held in his left hand. They looked like jellied fish eggs, glossy but inedible. "Mariah!" Lucius's voice burned against my face.

"You told me you loved olives," I said in a monotone. I felt as if time had slowed abruptly with this new understanding, and yet, still it made no sense to me. Why would he feel a need to drug my food and my drinks? I was a willing partner for him, why would he do that? There was no need. What was I missing here?

He set the glass of cherries on the table. "You finished your drink!" Again I had surprised him. "You drank that awfully fast," he said with a sly grin, surprised but obviously pleased. I stared down at him as he seated himself with his back to the dance floor. The floor was crowded with gyrating bodies. Suddenly the space began to glow and hum, and again I felt beckoned, drawn forth. Understand, Mariah, a voice from within my own heart told me, this has little to do with Lucius. "Let's dance," I demanded.

Lucius stood and followed me out to the dance floor. We danced apart to a strong bass beat. I watched him carefully as he looked upward toward the mezzanine. I let my eyes float to the ceiling as well. The balcony was crowded with men, some laughing, some chatting, but all stealing glances down toward the dance floor. I was startled to see familiar faces: one of the local news anchors, the Superintendent of Public Instruction, the Speaker of the Assembly. Then striding up to chat with a senator or two, came actor Hark Robinson, star of Showtime's Emmy-winning series *Chicago Chase*, and People Magazine's Sexiest Man Alive. I must have gasped; I couldn't help it. Lucius pulled me toward him right then, locking me into a traditional dance stance, his mouth near my ear. "Why do you keep looking up there?" he asked in an annoyed tone. "You can't see anything."

He was so condescending that I lost it. "Oh yeah?" I blurted. "Well it so happens I can see well enough to know Hark Robinson is up there!"

He jerked me back swiftly to look at my face, then he abruptly bent his head back, squinting in what to his eyes was very dim light. His reaction scared me. This was something I wasn't supposed to know. I shouldn't have tipped my hand.

"How do you know that?" he drilled.

I took a deep breath. "He's famous! Everybody knows what he looks like. I've seen him on so many talk shows, commercials, SNL--I can recognize him from the way he moves. Can't you?"

He glanced up again. "Oh, yeah," he said, sounding relieved. "You're right." He kept his grip on me, but he continued to stare upward for what seemed like several minutes. I was getting increasingly nervous, but I knew I couldn't leave yet. Something needed to happen here, I just wasn't sure what.

Lucius finally looked down at me, smiling and reasserting his boyish charm. "Do you want to meet him? Do you want to meet Hark?"

I looked up at him cautiously. I knew I was supposed to be impressed. "Oh," I breathed, trying to inject a bit of exhilaration into my voice. "You know Hark Robinson?"

"He's one of my clients," Lucius bragged.

"Hark Robinson ain't no farmer!"

"That shows what you know," Lucius boasted, on top again. "He owns significant acreage planted in avocado and sunflowers. Down south. It's an investment."

"Oh!" That was interesting, but truth be told I didn't want to meet this actor, no matter how famous he was. I wanted to leave, but could I leave yet? Maybe I was wrong about this urgent premonition making me feel like something more was supposed to happen. Maybe it was silly.

Lucius abruptly grabbed my hand. "We're going upstairs now," he informed me, and he pulled me off the dance floor.

He tugged my arm rather roughly, and I have to confess I was naive enough to be surprised. He led me toward the kitchen and onto a wide service elevator. The thing was big enough to hold a piano. By this point I was really wishing I'd gone home before Lucius even arrived at the coffee house. But you can't get off the roller coaster in the middle of the ride. The rumbling door slid open and we stepped into the room.

The walls up here were lined with plush looking booths, upholstered in suede and velvet. The colors were muted and rich, brown and salmon pink. The booths were huge, with bench seats long enough for a tall man to lie down on, and some of them had opaque curtains drawn across to hide activity within. Yes, I was naive, but there was no mistaking what these booths were designed for.

Lucius led me up to Hark Robinson and thrust me in front of him. "Mariah," he said simply. The actor leered at me, licking his lips. "Mariah," he repeated.

I was startled by the simplicity of the introduction, that everyone around me seemed to have forgotten their manners. I extended my hand. "It's nice to meet you, Mr. Robinson," I said politely. He took my hand, and laughed heartily, looked above my head and addressed Lucius. "Oh, she's a live one, all right, young and pretty. She'll do. She most certainly will do." He dropped my hand abruptly, not even looking at me. He reached around me to shake Lucius's hand. "The usual arrangement, sir?" Lucius asked him, and Hark nodded. "Bill me," he said.

I felt like I was going to vomit. "What the hell is going on here?" I said, finding it hard to keep my voice low.

The two men laughed again. "Get her another drink," Hark said to Lucius, and Lucius flagged down a waiter. "Gin martini. No olive."

I became aware that the speaker of the assembly was standing at Hark's left hand. A young woman had just been brought up and delivered to him as well. This girl was taller than me, in pink pumps and a mini skirt. Her eyes looked glazed over and she swayed in her heels. Her top kept pulling up, exposing her pierced belly button. She had a smile plastered unnaturally on her face. The speaker and another man were talking around her, just as Lucius and Hark were talking around me. But she didn't mind. Her eyes shifted back and forth from face to face, and she nodded and cooed, "Mmmm hmmm," at every comment and murmur the men made.

Hark Robinson laid a possessive hand on my arm, and another on my back. "We're going to the booth now to have another little drink," he commanded. I could see Lucius scurrying away like the rat that he was. I twisted away from the actor. "I am not going anywhere with you! You ought to be ashamed of yourself! You play a school teacher on TV for Christ's sake!" Hark stepped back, and I could see now that every eye in the place was fixed in my direction.

"What the hell is going on?" Hark yelled, and two waiters rushed over, looking like they wanted to grab hold of me. I lifted my hands and raised my elbows to ward them off. "Don't you touch me," I screamed. "I am going to leave this disgusting building now, and I am taking my friend with me." I lunged forward and grabbed the drugged girl away from the assembly speaker.

One waiter managed to grab my other arm. He leaned close to my ear. "You don't know what you're dealing with, girlie," he taunted like a schoolyard bully.

I pulled around to face him. "Are you threatening me?" I twirled back around. "Mr. Speaker," I said. "Will you be a witness to this? Will you allow this to happen?"

The Speaker looked at me agape that he had been recognized. I stepped closer to him. "You can't send one of your aides down to Auburn Boulevard to pick up an honest working woman and pay her a decent wage to service your appetite? No, you come here to this cheap and tawdry place and you abuse young women who have been drugged. This is shameful!" I was nearly crying by now, outraged and scared too. "Please let us leave here. Please guarantee our safety."

Everyone stepped back as I took the other woman's hand. "We're leaving now," I told her. She followed me willingly to the elevator. I pressed the button and the wide door slowly slid open. A tall burly man was getting off with two more young women with glazed eyes. They were thin and hipless, barely high school age. I wanted to grab them too, but I sensed that we should get out while the going was good. I tightened my grasp on the arm of my new friend, and we stepped into the large gaping hole that was the elevator.

It seemed to take forever to get to the ground floor. We stood stiffly, our arms linked. I reminded myself to breathe deeply. I thought of Craig, telling me I was protected. We are safe, we are safe, I chanted in a whisper, but my mind kept throwing up images of the long narrow hallway that led to the exit. Would we be able to traverse it undisturbed?

The elevator car landed with a thud, and my companion, still groggy, nearly fell over. I managed to help her regain her balance as the door opened. We stepped into a noisy kitchen. A half dozen faces atop stained chef's smocks stared at us. "Aqui!" a man's voice yelled into the void, and I glanced in the direction of the shout. The homeless man with the high cheekbones stood in a doorway across the room, waving and beckoning us toward him. "Praise God," I murmured, so happy I nearly burst into tears. "C'mon," I told my friend and we scrambled toward this unexpectedly close escape hatch. The man had apparently just received the handout of a bowl of soup, but he dropped it in the alley to help us escape. He threw his arms around us as we rushed over the threshold. "Run, mijas, run!" he cried and he raced with us down the alley toward the street. He turned us toward L and the Capitol. "Don't stop," he warned us. "Find a police officer. There are many in the park!"

We staggered across L Street, venturing into traffic even though the light was red. Cars were honking; drivers were yelling. We headed toward the Capitol that rose shining like a white beacon in the middle of a green oasis. Up the steps we scrambled, up to the giant doors, but it was very late, and of course they were locked. "Help, please, help," I shouted, feeling like Dorothy at the gates to the Wizard's palace in Oz. "Please let us in!"

A state police officer came rushing up the hallway, his hand on his gun holster. "Please, please!" I continued to yell. My companion had fallen to her knees, her forehead resting against the glass door.

"My friend," I pleaded as the officer drew near. He opened the door and thankfully let us in. He called an ambulance and he listened to my story. He insisted I go in the ambulance too, that a doctor should make sure I hadn't been drugged as well. I sat in the front with the driver. I knew I was fine. I really didn't want my family to know about this. I didn't want them to worry about me.

I guess the police raided the place. Sister Gabriel, who brought me my backpack, she told me that the officers who brought in my belongings had also brought in seven more drugged girls. She said the officers said the girls were alone in the building. The kitchen, the bar, the dance floor—all empty.

Chapter Eighteen
Rafa

Rafa paused. He'd been reading these newly discovered notebook passages aloud to Dale as they huddled around the small dining room table in his and Mariah's apartment. He took a deep breath. "The police were right: the place was closed down." Dale nodded solemnly.

After agitated phone conversations, first with a dispatcher then with a police detective, the officers had convinced Dale that the night club was a dead end in their search for Mariah. "Sir," the detective had said in a tone Dale recognized as midway between soothing and condescending, "I've got the report right here in front of me, and I don't see your sister's name. We've got uh, two, four, yeah—eight young women— most of them I interviewed myself—but there's nobody named Mariah Easter here in our records."

Now Dale stared at the tiny blue flowers on the tablecloth, so indicative of his sister's taste. "She was there that night," he said, sounding angry. "They messed up. Her name should have been in that report."

Rafa shrugged. "She gave them the slip, Dale. She was the only one who wasn't drugged and she got out of there." He stood up and took a step toward the kitchen. "What I don't get is why something like this didn't end up in the papers. Man! This is some hot story!"

Dale rose and followed Rafa to the refrigerator. "Those are some well-connected people she names there. They've got their ways."

Rafa opened the fridge, again tempted to grab a bottle of beer. Instead he picked up the package of string cheese and offered a stick to Dale. Mozzarella in hand, they headed back to the table. "I'm sorry, man," Rafa said as he reseated himself. "If only I'd searched a little harder I would have found this second notebook this morning before I called you. It would have saved us hours running around downtown."

"Stop blaming yourself, Rafa," Dale admonished him. "For all you know it's supposed to happen this way. For some mystical reason, maybe we're supposed to follow her footsteps."

Rafa looked up in surprise. If someone as cynical as Dale was talking about mysticism, then miraculous work was afoot. He picked up the notebook again. "Well, if that's the case," he said softly, "I guess we should head over to the hospital. That's what she talks about on the next page. She's sitting in the hospital cafeteria."

Dale snatched the notebook away from Rafa. "No, the next stop is my house. I cooked up a big pot of Jambalaya last night for Luisa and me, and you know what? It's even better the next day. You need a good meal, Rafa. I can tell." He stood up. "C'mon."

Rafa trailed obediently after Mariah's older brother. "Okay, but give me back the notebook," he insisted. "I'm going to keep reading in the car."

Luisa

Luisa and Dale lived in a Spanish style house near William Land Park. Luisa loved to dig in the garden, a love she said began with Samantha's school garden so many years earlier. She could even remember a day when Dale's father Charlie came to school to help the kids swing a pick to break up the Bermuda grass thatch in the deserted field. She liked to recreate that early memory wherever she lived, planting a winter garden with spinach, broccoli, and big yellow and blue pansies. She also had a cutting garden with daisies and asters on the side of the house. She was there when Dale and Rafa drove up. When she caught sight of the sorrow on her younger brother's face, she immediately stepped forward to embrace him, holding him for a long time. Dale reached around them both and shepherded them into the house.

"You sit, Rafa," Dale commanded. "I'll get lunch ready. Tell Luisa where we've been and what we've done." Rafa sat down on their overstuffed couch and immediately poured his heart out to his sister. She had no iPad, no machine at her side to respond to him. She knew she didn't need it at that moment. She simply listened.

After a time, she went into the kitchen to check on Dale. She grabbed an iPad from the counter where she had left it. "Dale," she typed. "You are making us a feast!" He had re-heated the jambalaya, made a green salad with mushrooms and cauliflower and was now slicing apples and cheese. She bobbed her head, wondering what to say next, whether to tease, scold or praise him. All this food was unnecessary, but she knew it was how he handled emergencies, she knew he had to feel useful. She put down the iPad and hugged him tight. She began to rock slightly, because she knew he needed that rocking more than she did. She knew he needed to be able to locate himself here and now in the space of this kitchen.

Their arms still wrapped around each other, they moved back toward the living room to summon Rafa to lunch, but he was asleep on the couch. Dale chuckled and started to say his name, but Luisa tugged at his shoulder and shook her head. They went back to the kitchen where Luisa had left her iPad. They sat at the built-in breakfast nook, overlooking their big back yard.

"I'm sure Rafa got almost no sleep last night," Dale conceded as he looked at all the food he had prepared.

"Rafa needs his sleep," Luisa agreed. "Rafa always trouble sleeping."

She handed the iPad to Dale and he typed in response. "ALWAYS?"

Luisa nodded, then commenced typing again. "When tiny boy, Rafa have night terrors. He wake up everyone in house with high-pitched screaming. Nearly every night!"

"He must have gone through something awful in his home country!" Dale typed.

"Yes, but Mama never found out what it was. Adoption agency didn't know, orphanage didn't know, and Rafa not talk. He claimed not to remember, and he claimed he not remember dreams. He says he no have dreams."

"That's weird," Dale typed. "I thought I'd read that everyone dreams."

"True," Luisa confirmed. "Everyone dreams. Rafa holds something deep inside. Mama took him therapists when he was little. He learned trust us, both awake and asleep. And then he rest better. Night terrors stopped. Mama knew he would get up in night and wander through house, but she felt he should have license to do as he pleased in his own home. She wanted him secure enough to wander if he wanted. So because of Mama's patience and effort, Rafa became more peaceful. But I can sense secrets that Rafa isn't even aware of. He's buried them very deep."

She looked at Dale and saw how tired he looked too. "Eat," she signed with American Sign Language. "We need you." Her movements were emphatic and jerky, thumping her chest hard as she signed "we." Dale smiled and shrugged. Luisa pushed her plate toward him, and he dished up jambalaya and salads for her and for himself.

Chapter Nineteen
Mariah's Journal

I had finished my hamburger, and was about to go get dessert when I saw a figure in a very odd costume. I couldn't tell at first if this person was a man or a woman, but he/she appeared to be wearing a hazmat suit!

The person in question was quite short, so I wasn't sure if it was a child or a small adult. And seeing anyone roaming around a hospital in such protective garb, well, it led my mind to all sorts of wild scenarios and questions, not the least of which was: "What do you know that I don't?" and "Do I need one of those outfits too?"

The person headed in front of me toward the counter, and appeared to be eyeing the candy bars and donuts. I followed because the soft serve machine was right there amid the other sweets. I couldn't help but stare. I know it's not polite, but in this day and age, when people are piercing their noses and tattooing their cheeks and necks, my motto is: if you don't want people to stare, then you better learn to blend in.

As I approached I could see that the person inside the suit was a young teen, just beginning to develop hips and breasts. She had long straw colored hair pulled into a fat braid. But the startling thing was that she wore a kind of *Phantom of the Opera* half mask inside her hooded plastic bubble. I assumed it was her Halloween costume. It had quite the spooky effect.

She was struggling to pull back some kind of Velcro at her wrists, apparently to free her hands from their plastic mittens. She seemed to be having quite a time, so I sidled up to her and spoke softly. "Do you need help with that?" I asked. "Can I help you?"

I was afraid I might startle her because her hood blocked her peripheral vision, but she seemed quite aware that I was there, almost as if she had summoned me herself. "Yes, thank you," she said, sounding a bit stilted. "That's very kind of you." She extended her right hand toward me. "If you lift the yellow band at my wrist, you'll see the Velcro that needs to be separated." I did as she told me, exposing her hand and wrist. The skin on the back of her hands was red and white like a candy-striped camellia, but it was blotched with brown patches, clusters of brown freckles and three black ulcerous wounds. I felt a stab of horror in my throat. My gaze flew immediately to her face, and I could see that the skin on her exposed cheeks and chin was much the same as her hands. I felt the bile rise in my mouth, wondering what might be hidden under her mask.

"You know what would be good?" she said enthusiastically as she opened the glass door and pulled out a large glazed donut with her free hand. "Ice cream on top of this donut!"

I laughed. "That does sound good." I figured this was only a half lie because normally I'd think this was a great idea, but looking at this poor girl's skin more or less took my appetite away.

"Do you want to split a donut with me?" she asked. "We could make two sundaes that way."

"Oh, no, thank you," I said, shaking my head. "I just ate a big hamburger, so I'm going to settle for a small dish of the soft serve. But I can help you make yours, if you want."

"Sure," she agreed. Then she shrugged in an exaggerated comical way. "Oh, no!" she said sarcastically. "Guess I'm going to have to eat the whooooole donut myself!"

I had to laugh.

We took our desserts and returned to the table where I'd left my backpack. We sat down across from each other, our spoons poised to dig in. "My name is Mariah Easter," I introduced myself.

"I'm Ariel Snow," she told me.

"It's nice to meet you," I said as she removed her hood to eat.

"It's nice to be with you," she said. "But I'm sure we've met before."

"We have?" I asked doubtfully. I didn't want to say so, but I was pretty sure I would remember meeting someone like Ariel.

"If not in this lifetime, then perhaps a previous one. Or maybe," she continued gleefully as she pounded her spoon into the ice cream and donut, "maybe we're energetic sisters."

I stared at her for a moment, wondering if a girl so young believed these things or if she was saying them to shock me in some way. She seemed a little too happy for hanging in a hospital in the middle of the night. I sampled a spoonful of ice cream. So cool and familiar and innocent.

I decided to take a chance. "When I first saw you pass by my table, I thought you were wearing a Halloween costume," I told her.

She laughed. "I guess that would be a logical deduction at this time of year," she admitted, still cheerful. Then she narrowed her red eyes and gave me a mischievous smile. "But you don't think it's a Halloween costume now? What do you think now?"

Oh, she was a clever girl--or maybe I should say she was a little smart ass! Of course I was hoping that my oblique reference to her outfit would lead her to explain her ailment to this curious mind of mine. Was it rude of me to want to know? Maybe I was prying where I shouldn't have gone, but there was no turning back now. I faced her challenge. "Well now," I answered straight forward, "I assume this is some kind of protective gear. You seem to have a problem that affects your skin."

She looked me square on, her eyebrows raised. "Yes, I am a Child of the Night!" she declared. "Does that scare you?"

I looked at her, unflinching. When I responded I wanted to make my voice sound kind, rather than challenging. I cleared my throat. "Do you want to scare me?" I asked.

She laughed again. "I don't want to scare anybody, but I often do! It's my fate, I guess, so I may as well enjoy it."

"That must be painful," I said.

"What?" she said as she shoveled in a large spoonful of ice cream and donut. "These leeches on my hands and face?"

"Well, yes, I'm sure those would be painful. But I was referring to the emotional pain--of knowing that people find your appearance frightening."

She sat chewing and digesting my words, I think. She wasn't laughing now, and I felt a little bad that I may have ruined her mood. Finally she swallowed, and looked over at me, a forced little smile on her lips. "So you don't think I'm a vampire or a werewolf or some other creature that roams around after dark? Because I am, you know. I am a night creature."

She seemed so young and so unhappy right then, all I wanted to do was please her. "Well," I said tentatively, "I guess I thought vampires and werewolves were stories somebody made up. But if you are a creature of the night--well, I'd certainly be interested in learning about that."

She sat up a little straighter in her chair and squared her shoulders. "They call me child of the night. I hide from the sun because I have a genetic abnormality. See, my genes are different from most other people's. If I go out in the sun, my skin gets burnt and damaged and it doesn't repair itself. Other people get burnt and then their skin heals up, but mine doesn't. I'm like a vampire. I can't go out in the sun, unless I'm wearing this get-up."

I watched her carefully as she spoke. She didn't sound sad or ashamed as she described her disability. Indeed she sounded rather proud.

"I may be weak in the day light," she continued, "but at night I become strong. I go out in the dark and I play basketball and swim. Even at one or two in the morning. I go hiking and I see owls and bats and coyotes. The night is an amazing place."

I nodded. I too was learning that the night was an amazing place. "This genetic difference you were talking about," I said, a little worried I was venturing unwelcome into private territory, "do you mind my asking what it's called?"

"It's called Xeroderma pigmentosum," she rattled off quickly. "It's also called XP because the official name is such a big mouthful."

"It must be quite rare," I said.

"Very," she said with an exaggerated nod. "Just my twin sister and me. We're the only ones who have it in our family."

There was a small tug of sadness behind my eyes. "Your sister has it too?" I repeated, hoping I'd heard her wrong.

She nodded. "That's why I'm here at the hospital. She's in a room upstairs. My parents are with her now. She's not doing very well." I felt my mouth drop open, unsure of what to say. "My parents like to come in the middle of the night to see her. We've all become such ghost owls, you know, it's how we live."

"Ghost owls?" The reference startled me. "What do you

mean, ghost owls?"

"Oh, you know," she said in that teasing little smart ass tone again. "People are either morning larks or ghost owls. They like to get up early in the morning, or they like to stay up late at night. Like you and me. We're ghost owls."

"Don't you mean night owls?" I asked.

She rolled her eyes. "I like to say ghost owls," she said. "That's what Native Americans call barn owls because they're nearly white and as quiet as moths. I like that. It sounds mysterious."

I stared at her, still searching for words. She finished her ice cream.

"Do you come here often?" she asked. "You weren't here last night."

"I have been here before," I said slowly, thinking of the morning my father died two and a half years earlier. "But it's been a long time." She gave me a disappointed look, so I jumped in again. "I really like their food here. Maybe--"

"Yeah," she agreed. "Maybe I'll see you here again." She lumbered to her feet awkwardly in her bulky suit.

"I hope so, Ariel," I said quickly. "And I hope your sister gets better."

She looked down at her hands and shook her head. "She's not going to get any better. That's just how it is." Her voice broke a little and she grasped her hood and swung it back over her head. "Thanks, Mariah! It's been real!"

I swallowed hard and batted back a few tears. "Yeah, reality," I murmured to myself. "It's a real bitch."

Chapter Twenty
Mariah's Journal

The next evening I went to visit Dale and Luisa. I wanted to tell someone about what had happened the night before at the club, and I didn't want to worry mom or upset Rafa, so Dale was going to be my designated listener. I rang the doorbell and Dale answered with a big basket of candy in his arms and a big grin on his face. He gave me an unwelcome grimace. "Hey, I was expecting neighborhood kids. The least you can do is say 'trick or treat!'"

"Oh, my God!" I exclaimed. "Is it Halloween? It is, isn't it? I can't believe I forgot!"

He stepped aside so I could walk through the door. "You forgot Halloween?" he said, as surprised as I was. Luisa was sitting on the couch by the front window, diligently watching for visitors to come up their path. "Luisa," Dale continued, "you should have seen this girl when she was younger. She'd be working on her Halloween costume for months: black cat, fairy princess, Glenda the good witch. She was even Harry Potter one year! But now she can't even remember it's Halloween. What has college life done to you, little sister? You can't take time off from studying for one night of fun? I can't believe you don't have a party to go to, or a dance club or costume parade in midtown or something. It's just--unbelievable."

Luisa was giggling, though still sneaking furtive glances out the front window. I sat beside her but she barely looked at me. Suddenly she squealed and the doorbell rang. She held up three fingers, and a quick look out the window confirmed that she was indicating the number of children on the porch. Dale held out his hand to her. "Come with me to the door," he invited, but she squealed again and shook her head. Dale went to the door without her.

"You don't want to go to the door?" I asked.

She shook her head and signed "No," but again she resumed her vigil at the window.

Dale came back and sat in a chair opposite us. "Luisa thinks she might scare the kids if she gets too excited," Dale explained.

She nodded and pointed again out the window. "But see," Dale said as he stood, waiting for the doorbell to ring. "She loves to see the kids all dressed up."

Luisa finally picked up her iPad as Dale again went to the door. "Dale thinks I would strike a blow for liberty if I answer the door for trick or treaters. As if I score a point for people with disabilities everywhere! Like I have the right to scare children on Halloween by squealing and gyrating in delight at their lovely costumes! It's not necessary. It's a night for the children. I like to see how happy they are, and I can see that fine through the window. This isn't a night for disability awareness!"

She let me read her statement and then she grabbed the iPad back as Dale returned to his chair. Quickly she deleted the entry. "What?" Dale asked, a bit suspicious at leaving two women alone to their own devices.

I had to laugh. "I'm sure she didn't tell me anything she hasn't said to you already!" Luisa pointed at me, and nodded emphatically, a definite "Yeah, what she said."

Dale looked at both of us annoyed. I lifted my hands in a defensive posture. "Hey, I'm not getting in the middle of this." Luisa tapped me on the shoulder, indicating that I was missing something on the porch. Two kids dressed as Disney's Beauty and the Beast were ringing the bell. "Wow," I said. "Very authentic." Luisa nodded. Dale went to the door.

I turned back around when Dale returned and for the first time I saw that the house was decorated with carved pumpkins and skulls painted with bright fuchsia, green and orange paint. There were pots of orange and yellow mums and white candles set on every available surface. The house looked like a church or plaza ready for a fiesta. I was entranced. "Is all this for Halloween?" I asked.

"No," Dale said, "for Day of the Dead."

"Dia De Los Muertos!" Luisa typed quickly and showed me her iPad. Then she jumped up, grabbing my hand and pulling me with her. She took me into the dining room where the built-in sideboard was filled with lit candles, orange flowers and photos of people and animals. The biggest display was reserved for framed photos of my father, showing him at different stages of his life: as a boy, as a young man with toddler Dale, holding me and standing with my mother at their wedding, and finally a portrait with all of us together taken shortly before he died.

"This is our Dia De Los Muertos altar," Luisa typed. "We have placed here in the care of the universe the people we love who have dropped their bodies and moved on in their journeys." Looking at the photos of Daddy I felt myself starting to tear up. I thought also of Ariel's sister, and wondered what side of the divide she was on now. I also thought of my mother, and wondered how she was doing. I hadn't talked to her in several days.

I looked up and saw two additional photos on the altar. One of Dale and one of Luisa. "Why are your pictures here too?" I asked her.

She gave me a small smile as she picked up the photo of my brother. "We have placed these here to symbolize that we are leaving behind our lives as single people. We are grateful for the time we spent and the things we learned as solitary beings, but now we are joined as one, and this coming year we will take vows to affirm that."

I threw my arms around Luisa to embrace her. "What a wonderful affirmation. I love that!"

She squealed and broke free, then reached over to pick up a tiny doll, no bigger than her pinky finger that was set between the two photos. She rested her hand on my arm as she typed. "This symbolizes our decision not to have children. This symbolizes the death of a dream, especially for Dale. It was hard for both of us to let go of this dream, but we both knew it was the right decision to make." She tightened her grip on my arm and I could see she was shaking. Cold tears were running down my cheeks. She put down the doll, and we slipped into a warm hug.

The doorbell rang and I heard the door swing open. "Oh, gee, Luisa! Where are you? You've got to see this!"

Luisa pulled back and looked at me, obviously torn about whether or not she should go to the door. "C'mon, Lu!" Dale shouted. "You don't want to miss this."

Keeping a tight grip on my waist, Luisa walked slowly toward the door. I stood beside her, my hand and arm steadying her as we moved forward. We approached the door, as if we were bracing ourselves for bad news, as if we were afraid. "Tell us first," I called to Dale. "Tell us what they look like--so we won't be startled."

Luisa froze, nodding at Dale and then turning to nod at me. She liked this idea, she could see the wisdom in it. Dale laughed. "It's one of your favorite movies, Lu! And guess what--yours too, Mare!"

Luisa turned to me with a surprised grin. We stepped forward and stood in front of the open door. Before us was the cast of the Wizard of Oz--the scarecrow, tin man, lion, the green-faced wicked witch, Glenda, and of course Dorothy who stood holding a real live cairn terrier. They were all adults, obviously out for a lark as they rattled their fund-raising cans for UNICEF. The Scarecrow tapped his foot, counted to four, and the assemblage burst into a low-pitched version of *Off to See the Wizard.* When I heard the deep voices, I realized that this group of characters were all men in drag! Luisa burst out laughing, and she looked no different than any other woman having fun on a holiday. I was laughing too, but I kept having to wipe tears that were leaking out of my eyes. I realized then that I didn't want to spoil the evening by burdening my brother with my sad stories. Another night maybe.

Chapter Twenty-One
Mariah's Journal

When I left Dale and Luisa's house I drove around their neighborhood looking at Halloween decorations. I headed up Land Park Drive to Broadway and I stopped at the Tower Cafe. I was just killing time. I ordered tea and a cookie. I didn't even want the cookie. I got out my journal and caught up on all the events of the past few days. At midnight I headed over to Mercy Hospital.

The cafeteria was nearly deserted as I strolled in. I saw Ariel sitting at the same table we'd shared the night before, her head and hands exposed as she ate a donut sans ice cream. Her head bobbed up as I entered, and she lifted a hand to wave and call to me. "Mariah!" she called, grinning, obviously pleased to see me. That felt good.

"Hi," I said simply as I seated myself across from her. "No ice cream tonight?"

She snorted and smiled. "No, not tonight. Guess I've already overdone it on the treats. Still had room for a donut though. Can't get through the day without a donut or two."

I restrained myself from making a joke that maybe she'd make a good police officer. "Did you go trick or treating?" I asked.

"No-oo!" She stretched the word into two syllables as if to emphasize the indignation of her response. "I am fourteen years old," she declared. "I am wa-ay too old for trick or treating. I mean, really, did *you* go trick or treating?"

"Hey, if I had remembered that it was Halloween, I might have gone!" I said, conjuring up my own righteous indignation.

"I mean, dressing up and getting free candy—what's not to like?"

She rolled her eyes. "You forgot it was Halloween?" she asked.

I sighed. "Yeah, I've been kind of an airhead lately."

She laughed. "That happens sometimes," she agreed. "Especially if you've been hanging out in a hospital."

"How's your sister?" I asked.

She shrugged. "The same." She paused, pursing her lips together, and we both sat silent. "Do you want part of my donut?" she offered.

"No, I'll get something in a minute, maybe. I've had a lot of candy already tonight."

"Oh, yeah?" she said. "Where'd you get all the candy if you didn't remember it was Halloween?"

"Oh, I went to my brother's house and he and his fiancée had the place all fixed up for the trick-or-treaters. They had lots of candy there."

She nodded, taking another bite. "It must be nice to have a brother. I just have a sister."

I swallowed hard, realizing it would be inappropriate for me to express any jealousy that she had a sister when I only had a brother. After all, she soon would have no siblings at all. "Can I ask you something?"

"I guess," she said.

I took a deep breath, bracing myself for tears, anger or smart ass retorts. "If you didn't go trick or treating, and this suit isn't your Halloween costume, then why are you wearing it? I mean it's dark now; you don't need any protection from the sun because the sun has set for the day. So why wear the suit?"

She stared at me with her bloodshot eyes, her mouth drawn into a straight line. "I like this suit, okay?"

"It is a cool suit," I blurted, then I stopped myself realizing how silly that sounded, how it could be taken a couple ways. Actually the damn thing looked really hot and uncomfortable. But she was giving me a small smile, as if my comment hadn't bothered her.

"I feel powerful in this suit," she said, feigning a bit of bravada as she raised her chest and squared her shoulders.

"You look powerful in it," I agreed with a smile and a nod.

She looked down at her donut. "Uh huh. And the other thing is that people can't see much of my skin when I'm wearing this suit. They really look shocked and stare at me when they see my skin. But in this suit, they can't see. They still stare at me, but I can just stare right back at them. I give them a big fierce look--like this." She scrunched her mouth and her eyes together in as mean a bulldog look as she could muster.

"Impressive!" I said.

She rolled her eyes again. "No, it's not. You're not scared of me."

"No, I'm not scared, but you've been nice to me. We've only just met, but we've gotten to know each other a little bit, so--you know--I don't think you're all that scary. But I think you could easily scare people if you want to." I paused and we stared at each other. "If you want to," I repeated.

She held the last bit of donut between her thumbs and index fingers. "I don't know," she said. "It's not that I want to scare anybody. But sometimes they do look scared when they look at me." She paused. "I don't know. I guess I'd rather scare them with my suit."

"That makes sense," I told her.

"Do you think so?" she asked eagerly. I nodded. "That's good. Thanks." She stuck the last of her donut in her mouth and chewed thoughtfully. "I probably should go," she said. "My parents are probably wondering where I am."

"See ya, Ariel," I told her.

"Happy Halloween, Mariah."

Chapter Twenty-Two
Luisa

Luisa bent over her lunch plate, pushing around the cauliflower and mushrooms with her fork. "You're awfully quiet," Dale said softly. Usually they typed as they ate, enjoying long leisurely meals.

She sat up suddenly, her mouth filled with raw vegetables. She circled her index finger around her forehead to indicate that she wasn't merely thinking, she was ruminating. After chewing and swallowing she turned to her iPad. "I have an idea. Not sure it's a good idea, but going to do it anyway."

Dale didn't take the time to type in response. "And this idea is?" he verbalized.

She rocked and laughed, slapping her fingers together in the American Sign Language sign for "Doesn't matter." She didn't want Dale to concern himself, but she knew it was his nature to worry. He narrowed his eyes and pursed his lips: his own brand of nonverbal communication, a look she recognized as a warning to think before she acted. She squealed softly. "Don't worry," she typed. "Relax and finish your lunch."

She got up and went to retrieve her assistive communication device with the robotic voice. As she began to program it, she saw Dale throw up his hands. "I'm not going to watch!" he exclaimed, and she gave him a grateful smile. He grabbed Mariah's notebook and sat down with his iPad. Luisa saw him log on to the internet. She was satisfied he was elsewhere occupied.

She took her device and went into the living room where Rafa slept on the couch. She leaned over and tapped him on the chest, then activated her robotic voice. "Rafa!" the machine exclaimed. "Tell me what you are dreaming. Right now!"

Rafa jerked awake. "What?--oh! Luisa. . ."

"Tell me what you are dreaming," the robot repeated.

"Mariah, I was dreaming about Mariah! She was with this woman--oh my God--Luisa!" His face crumpled and his jaw began to quiver. "Luisa, Mariah was with my mother!"

"Maaa," Luisa vocalized.

"No, no, not with Mom, not our mother Anna. My birth mother. I saw her. I recognized her face."

Luisa immediately sat down on the couch and embraced her brother. "Maaa," she vocalized again, unable to control her voice. She leaned back, frustrated with herself. "More," she signed frantically.

Rafa shook his head. "I don't know any more."

Luisa typed quickly into her machine. "You do know," the robot said. "Picture her. More will come." He silently stared at her, so she continued typing. "Now. Before you lose it."

He swallowed. "Okay." He leaned back on the couch and closed his eyes.

"Mother," Luisa's robot said. "What she look like?"

"She has long wavy hair." Rafa opened his eyes and leaned toward his sister. "Luisa, I think she may be African. She has big brown eyes and full lips." He closed his eyes again. "She's really beautiful."

"Do you see anyone else?" Luisa asked with her robot.

"Yes," Rafa said, his voice shaking. "There's a man there. He has heavy eyebrows and a visored cap. He has a gun. My mother is screaming; she's telling me to run and hide. But now Mariah is there. She thinks she can save my mother." Tears ran down Rafa's cheeks, but his voice was angry. "Mariah!" Again he opened his eyes. "She's so stupid sometimes, Luisa. She's had it so easy here, born in California. She's so naive, she doesn't understand how dangerous life can be sometimes."

Luisa draped her left arm around him, pulling his head onto her shoulder. Even still she continued typing with her right hand. "It's okay, Rafa. Important dream, but only a dream. Mariah and mother never met this lifetime. You worry about Mariah, so you dream her in danger. But we don't know."

He leaned back to look at her face. "Luisa, how can I be sure that this woman in my dream. . ." He paused to take a deep breath. "How can I be sure that really was my mother? That *that* was what she looked like? Maybe I'm imagining it."

Luisa nodded slowly and waved her hand downward in a calming motion, knowing it would take her a while to type something reassuring. "The moment I woke you up and you knew the dream, you were sure," her robot said finally. "It would be easy to talk yourself out of it. But in that moment, you knew. It was a certainty for you. Remember that feeling and trust it."

Rafa looked into her eyes and squeezed her hand. "I'm going to draw a picture of her. I'm not sure I can get a good likeness or not, but I have to try."

"Rafa, you will dream about her again," Luisa told him. "Know this is true and you will remember more and more."

Luisa turned and saw Dale standing in the doorway. "Ready for lunch yet?" Dale asked.

"Yeah," Rafa agreed with a sigh and a grin. "I am feeling pretty hungry."

They moved back into the kitchen, where Mariah's notebook sat on the table. "Have you been reading Mariah's journal?" Rafa asked Dale. "Learn anything useful?"

"Well, I have been reading," Dale said as he dished up Jambalaya from a pot on the stove. "I don't know if it will lead anywhere though."

Rafa accepted the plate and took a big bite before even sitting down. "What about that girl in the hospital she talks about?" he asked. "The one she met in the cafeteria?"

Dale leaned against the wall by the stove. He shrugged. "I felt I was grasping at straws, but well, a clue is a clue. So I googled the girl--Ariel Snow. I thought--who knows--maybe Mariah got to know her and her family a little bit."

"What did you find?" Rafa asked. "She and her family must live here in the area somewhere."

Dale looked down at the floor. He sighed and looked up. "Yeah. What I found was Ariel's obituary. She died the week after Halloween, just a few days after the death of her sister. Both from melanoma."

Chapter Twenty-Three
Mariah's Journal

I went to the hospital cafeteria a third night in a row. I was beginning to wonder how long I could keep up a schedule like this. But truth be told I was wondering in a kind of intellectual way; I really didn't feel unusually tired. Plus I seemed to be keeping up with my class work. It's as if my body had developed the ability to sustain itself on only three or four hours of sleep each night.

I didn't see Ariel when I walked in, so I sat down at our usual table and pulled out my copy of Hamlet that I need to finish reading before we see Branagh's movie version next week. I was just about to open it to the first act, when I caught sight of a girl dressed simply in jeans and sweatshirt in a corner near the garbage cans. It was Ariel in real life, without her big hazmat suit. I grabbed my things and went over to join her.

She was holding her typical glazed donut, but she wasn't eating. She was squeezing it, and breaking it into little pieces. She didn't even look up when I approached. "Hey, Ariel," I said. "Are you okay?"

She glanced in my direction and gave me a wan little smile. "You recognized me without my space suit," she said. "I wondered if you would."

"I didn't at first, but the donut was a give-away," I told her with a smile.

She nodded as I sat down. "My sister died this evening," she told me in a low voice. "I told my parents I needed to hang out here till way late, because I was afraid I wouldn't see you again, you know, since I don't really know who you are or where you live."

"Oh, Ariel, I'm so sorry about your sister. Here--" I reached into my backpack for a pen and notepad. "Let me give you my email address. Or we could be Facebook friends. Are you on Facebook?"

"That's okay, Mariah," she told me in a terse voice, then she seemed to realize how abrupt she sounded and she softened her tone. "I felt bad that I wouldn't get a chance to tell you goodbye."

I nodded, finally understanding. "Yeah," I said lamely. "I would have felt bad too."

"Mariah?" she interjected in a loud voice. "Why are you here? I mean here." She pointed down with both hands at the table where we sat. "Here in a hospital cafeteria in the middle of the night? Do you work here or are you visiting somebody? Or are you sick? Is that why you're here every night?"

I scratched my head. I wasn't sure I wanted to tell her how I ended up here two nights ago, and I was afraid she'd be embarrassed if I told her I kept coming back just to see her. "Oh," I said, "it's not important."

"No, Mariah, it is important," she said insistently. "You know what? I went home last night and realized that I did nothing but talk about myself for the past two nights, and I don't even know your story! I mean, nobody comes to a hospital in the middle of the night just to eat soft serve ice cream."

"Well this is probably the only place in town you can get soft serve ice cream in the middle of the night," I pointed out.

"Are you serious?" she asked sincerely. "Look, if that's why you come here, that's fine. Or if you don't want to tell me why you're here, that's fine too. But I felt really selfish, you know, because I wasn't being very nice. I was all wrapped up in my problems, but I wasn't asking you if you needed to talk about what's happening with you."

"Wow, Ariel, that's sweet," I told her.

"No, it's not. I was way late! I should have asked you right away. I'm really pretty selfish."

"Ariel, gee, don't be so hard on yourself," I said. "You've just had a terrible loss. You're entitled to be a little self-centered when you've been through something as awful as what you've gone through."

"Yeah, I guess," she admitted, then she lifted her head to look at me. "Are you going through something awful?" she asked me.

"No," I replied immediately. I was going through something very bizarre, but it wasn't awful. I couldn't call it bad. "I was at a party the other night, and this girl who I didn't even know got sick. I helped her come here to the hospital. That's all. Anyway, I've been coming back because--well, I found out it's a cool place to hang out. You know, the soft serve and all."

She smiled at me. I think she knew I was lying about that last. "You're like a Good Samaritan, Mariah. You bring somebody to the hospital and you don't even know them."

"I wasn't really being all that good," I whined. "I really needed to get away from that party and all. It's not a good story."

"I just wish I wasn't so selfish," she continued.

"Ariel!" I exclaimed. "Cut yourself some slack! And don't make me your role model! I've been pretty selfish myself this past month." I paused, maybe realizing that for the first time. I took a deep breath. "You know what? I think learning to be a

Good Samaritan or an unselfish person--it takes time. Sometimes it's work, but maybe it gets easier the older you get." I stopped again, feeling unworthy to give advice. "At least I hope it does. Don't be so down on yourself. Give yourself time."

"But Mariah," she said, her voice tearing, "I don't have that much time. I have to learn to be a better person now. Now is the only time I have!"

"Ariel," I blurted. "You don't have to learn to be a better person! You are unique in the universe: you're Ariel and you're perfect."

She squinted at my sudden enthusiasm. "Sure," she said, "but haven't you heard? YOLO! You only live once."

"Hey, weren't you the one who was rattling off stuff about past life incarnations that first night we met?" I reminded her.

She waved her hand and rolled her eyes. "I was just going on," she confessed. "I don't know if I believe in any of that. In fact, maybe I believe in nothing. Nothing!" She paused to grace me with a look of disgust. "What do you believe in?"

"Everything," I said.

She snorted at that, but couldn't hide a smile. "You can't believe in everything!" she said. "A lot of the stuff out there contradicts each other."

"Doesn't matter," I insisted. "I don't know if we go off to heaven when we die, or if we're reincarnated and do it all over again. The Hindus say there's a great Oversoul, and we all become one in that. Maybe that's what happens. I don't know, and it doesn't matter. I just know something happens, rather than nothing."

But Ariel was still being stubborn. "How can you be sure?" she asked me in her best tone of skepticism.

"Well, I can't be. I can't fill a beaker with chemicals and prove that God exists. But I know God is. Simply is. I just know."

"I want to know it," she said simply.

"And that's enough," I told her. "Let God and the universe take care of the rest for you."

She smiled. "Okay." She pulled out her cell phone to check the time. "My parents will be in the parking lot in a few minutes, so I've got to go."

"Ariel," I said, "the real reason I kept coming back here is because we're both ghost owls, and when you meet another ghost owl, well, you just want to hang out with them a little bit."

"I know," she said grinning. "That's true, huh?"

"Yeah."

"There's a donut shop we like to go to--my Dad and me. We like to get there when they open at 4:30 in the morning," she told me. "It's on Broadway at 27th."

Maybe I'll see you there," I told her.

"Yeah, see you around, Mariah." she said.

Chapter Twenty-Four
Mariah

It'd been over a month and I still had no idea why I have this bizarre gift. But following the energy seemed like a great idea after Ariel told me about her favorite donut shop. Instead of staying up late, I decided I could go to bed early, wake up when it was still dark, and go out exploring in the morning before dawn.

Funny thing was I woke up this morning craving donuts. It took me a minute to realize I'd been having that darn dream. I don't think I've had it at all these past two months. There I was, walking down that familiar hallway with a piddly little slice of cinnamon toast again. I felt so frustrated that I sat down determined to eat it myself! Oh, it smelled so good, my mouth was watering! I lifted the toast to my lips and took a hefty bite. I don't remember what it tasted like. After all it was a dream. Do we get cheated out of scent and taste in our dreams? I'm not sure, but I do know this: I took a bite, I chewed it up, I swallowed it, and then I felt so much better. As if I'd somehow been vindicated, released from my worries.

Then the radio snapped on, and the broadcaster was talking about the weather, how it'd been raining all night. I turned it off and pulled myself out of bed. Sure, the dream left me feeling peaceful, but hungry! I was primed for a sugary breakfast.

The donut shop was several blocks from our flat, but still it was a walk I knew I could make in 15 or 20 minutes at my usual gait. I went up to N Street and headed east. There was a row of palms lining this stretch of the road. They looked like jeweled towers.

I turned south on 24th since I knew it had an underpass beneath the WX freeway connector. The streets were quiet. The pale brick facade of CLARA Studios for the Performing Arts looked like it was made of soft fuzzy suede. An arching orange tree was weighted down with giant florescent orbs, mottled green and yellow as they slowly ripened. Persimmons throbbed spicy orange neon on a tree near the light rail station. A train slipped by, silent and long, a blur of silver and blue, like the Disney fairy in Pinocchio.

I walked under the freeway. Traffic was light but steady, and standing beneath the massive girders the whoosh of cars overhead could be imagined as rushing water tumbling over a cliff to a lake or river below. I leaned against the concrete, and for the first time I began to wonder what Yosemite Falls or China Cove Beach at Point Lobos would look like in the middle of the night with these new eyes of mine. I wondered if Rafa would drive with me to the coast at Thanksgiving break, just for a day or two. We could go to Point Reyes; it's close and I love it there. I was tempted to turn around and go home, to be there when Rafa woke up so I could tell him about how strange all this has been, and how I want to share it with him. Later today, I decided. I've kept this a secret for too long.

I stood up straight and continued heading south. At the edge of the underpass, in a clump of oleander bushes, I was startled to see a man asleep in a dark blue mummy bag. I nearly gasped when I saw the high cheekbones and neatly trimmed beard. It was the homeless man who had helped me escape from the nightclub. His face looked pale and serene in repose. I hastened on, not wanting to disturb him.

I quickly approached the McDonald's at the corner of 24th and Broadway. I was surprised to see it was open even at this early hour. Their drive-through window was busy, and the taillights of cars burst like shiny pomegranate seeds.

This stretch of Broadway was not very attractive, though we came here often when I was growing up. My father always said that Los Jarritos was the best Mexican food for the money in Sacramento. Mom liked to point out that once Daddy found Los Jarritos he stopped looking, so this endorsement was not all that well researched. But we all loved it anyway, so what did it matter? Mom loved the New Canton Cafe for its dim sum and it's moo shu shrimp. But there are also the fast food joints, the dingy-looking auto body shop, and the adult book and video stores. "Who needs to come to a store now that we've got the internet?" Daddy would say, and Mom would grab my hand and give his shoulder a little push. "I don't know," she'd mumble. "Just keep walkin'."

Finally I arrived at the tiny donut shop, shaped like a shoe box set on end, a stucco rectangle, painted a soft pale green. It was flanked by camellia bushes that were just beginning to bloom with blossoms that were white and watermelon red. The flowers looked as if they were beaded with glittery sequins and jewel-toned droplets of water. I lingered there at the entrance, heady with the scent of donuts, oily and sugary, mesmerized by the beauty of these camellias. They say Sacramento is the camellia capital, I recalled, and I felt suddenly happy at how lovely my world is.

I went inside and stood before the small glass counter under the florescent overhead lights. The donuts were displayed like jewelry, popping with pink, blue and white frosting, the shiny brown sheens of chocolate and maple, the glossy sugar glazes. I was perusing a treasure chest, and again I was enchanted by the wonder of my new vision. A tall man with tiny round glasses waited at the cash register. I ordered an old-fashioned donut and a cup of coffee and turned to sit at one of the two small tables, both square and Formica-topped.

I leaned against the plate glass window feeling a little sleepy. I was satisfied with this new schedule as the late nights were beginning to wear on me. This will be better I decided, you know--once I get used to it. I checked my phone for the time. It was 4:40. I wondered if Ariel and her father came here every day. No matter. If I came here every morning, I'd see them eventually. It had been three days since I'd seen Ariel at the hospital. I'd thought about her a lot, and I wondered how she was doing.

I held the paper coffee cup in both my hands to warm myself. It was chilly this morning. Traffic was beginning to pick up outside: huge sixteen-wheeler trucks and paneled vans making deliveries, Regional Transit buses and yellow taxis rumbling by like buzzing dragon flies.

The bell on the door rattled a greeting as three elderly people ambled through, each holding an object. The African American man held a newspaper, the Asian woman held a leather box, and the Caucasian man held a messenger's bag slung across his chest. They were very ordinary-looking in their sweat pants and heavy jackets, all bespectacled and graying, laugh lines softening their faces. But the light in the room increased as they entered, and I stared unabashed as I nibbled on my donut. I saw a golden glow emanating from their heads and chests. They seemed to share this light; the yellowish beams spun around their torsos, weaving them together. I glanced at their hands wondering about mundane connections: was the woman married to one of the men? Were the two men a couple? But they wore no rings to guide my assessment of their status. Their voices were low and initially indistinguishable one from the other. Not that I had a desire to eavesdrop, but they appeared a curious trio, and I couldn't help but wonder what their stories might be.

The man behind the counter greeted them by name--Al, Tim and Sally, I heard him say. They got a little louder as they exchanged pleasantries with the owner, laughing and making comments about the weather. They placed their order, got their donuts and settled in at the other table beside mine. Sally smiled at me as she took the chair that faced me. "G'morning," I murmured softly, and nodded. She smiled more broadly and announced, "Good morning!" in response. The two men turned to eye me then as if they hadn't been aware of me before. They smiled genially and said hello as well.

The owner brought them a pot of coffee and actual ceramic mugs for their table. Well, I thought. They're not just regulars, they're fixtures at this place. I sipped my own brew. It wasn't bad, but I was more of a tea drinker myself. Sally took a bite of pastry and a swallow of coffee, and then she opened her leather box. I leaned forward to see what might be inside. It was what appeared to be a finely made Chinese checkerboard. Tim, the Caucasian man, opened his messenger bag and pulled out a black velvet pouch. He handed it to Sally, and she slowly and meticulously began to remove the colored glass marbles: one at a time she set them on the board.

Al, the African American man, was unfolding the newspaper. He had his back to me, so I couldn't see his face, but I could see what he was reading in the newspaper. He turned immediately to the weather page, and he made a great production of refolding the crinkly crackly paper, so that it lay flat with no wrinkles or bulges. "Says it's going to rain on Monday," he said nonchalantly.

"They're wrong," Tim told him, and they all laughed.

"Says it's a La Nina year, and they're afraid that's going to aggravate the drought," Al said slowly.

"Now they're right about that," Tim said, and he and Sally nodded with pursed lips and furrowed brows.

"We may as well have sunny weather now while we can enjoy it," Sally said with a grin. "Don't you think so?"

"If you want the weather to be sunny, Sal, that's what we'll have," Tim agreed, patting her hand. But Al didn't respond, he was busy turning pages and wrestling with the folds of the newspaper as if it were a wild bird rather than an inanimate object. I saw he had turned to the obituaries.

"Ah," he noted with what seemed a touch of sadness. "Both those little girls passed together last week, within days of each other."

"Well, that's no surprise," Sally said in a matter of fact way, as if she were talking about passing the bar exam rather than dying. "They came in together, the two of them did, and they passed over together. That was planned." Tim nodded.

Al gave the newspaper another rough shake, folding it down to highlight one column. Suddenly he turned in his chair and thrust the newspaper toward me. "Did you see this?" he asked me. "Ariel and her sister Caitlin--they both passed."

I nearly dropped my cup of coffee. "What?" I asked. I couldn't believe that this stranger was speaking to me, I couldn't believe that he knew I was there to meet Ariel, and I couldn't believe that Ariel had died. Of course she had looked unhealthy, and she made it clear to me she had little time left, but I'd had no idea. "It's a shock, I know," Sally was saying, and I blinked at her, feeling confused, and wondering if finally I might wake up and realize that all this strangeness had been a dream.

"Do you need some more coffee?" Al asked, leaning forward to peek inside my paper cup. He turned back toward the counter. "Roger, give this girl a decent cup for crying out loud."

He stood up and Roger behind the counter humbly handed over a ceramic cup. Al filled the cup with hot coffee and placed it at the seat beside him at his own table. "Now c'mon over here and join us," he commanded.

I was still stunned, but never had the energy been clearer about where I needed to go. I picked up my half-eaten donut, my napkin and paper cup, and hastened over to the other table.

They introduced themselves. I didn't think it would be very polite to tell them I'd been eavesdropping and already knew their names, but if I had, I don't think they would have been surprised.

I wondered if they already knew my name, but I told it to

them anyway. "How did you know?" I asked.

"What?" Al said with a mischievous smile. Tim and Sally stared at me too, chins lowered and eyebrows raised, waiting for me to finish the question, as if the question itself was a type of test.

I wondered how to phrase it most effectively. "How did you know--well, that I would be interested in Ariel's obituary? How did you know that I knew her?"

Al waved his hand dismissively. "That's an easy one. You tell her, Tim."

Tim rolled his eyes and gave a mock bow to Al, as if sarcastically thanking him for the honor of getting to show off some knowledge. "As soon as we came into the shop this morning, Mariah, we could all see Ariel's energy signature on you. We knew she had sent you here. We don't know what significance that has for any of us--"

"We don't know?" Al interrupted. "Speak for yourself, old man!"

Sally laughed as Tim shook his head at Al's admonishment. "Al is Oscar the Grouch's grandfather!" she teased. "Do you detect a family resemblance?"

I laughed and Al showed he was a good sport. "It's true. I live in a garbage can in an alley two blocks down by the Taco Bell!"

"You wish!" Tim exclaimed. "It'd probably be better than going home and eating your own lame cooking."

Again the table rocked with laughter, but I still felt disoriented and throbbing with the pain of losing my new young friend so quickly. Sally leaned forward and touched my arm. "We loved Ariel too, dear," she said. "We don't mean to appear disrespectful."

"Oh, I know," I said quickly. "I understand." There followed a long silence as they all looked at me, perhaps waiting for another question.

"Um," I said tentatively, and all three of them leaned forward. I considered my words carefully. "Tim," I began, "you said you could see Ariel's energy signature on me. What does that mean?"

"We all have our own energy signature," Tim explained. "It's the part of the individual that we take from incarnation to incarnation. In each life cycle, we will experience different genders and ethnicities, different stations in life, different biochemical make-ups, aptitudes and abilities. But the energy signature doesn't change."

"What does it look like?" I asked. "How could you tell I was a friend of Ariel's?"

"Oh, no, Mariah," Tim continued, "it isn't just that you're a friend of Ariel's. That's not what we're talking about. You're a member of the same cluster as Ariel, like members of the same tribe."

"You see," Sally said, "within each cell of our vehicles--our bodies—there's DNA. There's the physical DNA--which is unique to each person, then there's the magnetic DNA--which is identical for members of each cluster or tribe, and finally there's the crystalline DNA--and that is the Divinity we all share."

"She asked what it looks like," Al said in his crotchety way. "Don't forget to answer the question!"

"That's a harder question," Tim said. "Maybe you'd like to take that one yourself, Al."

But Al shook his head. "I think you can handle it, Professor!"

Tim bowed again to Al, then turned back to me. "Different people see it different ways. Some people see it as colorful waves of light. That's how I see it, and that's very common. But some people hear tones like musical notes, others smell particular scents or odors that no one else can smell. I've heard some people may even get a taste in their mouth when they encounter folks from their own clusters. But it may not help them distinguish other clusters, just recognize their own people. And Sally--well, you want to tell Mariah how you detect energy signatures, Sal?"

"Well, it doesn't happen all the time, just with advanced spirits like yourself, I see a picture of one kind or another, a bird or an animal, or perhaps a flower or tree. I even met a woman once who conjured up the image of a raging river for me."

This made me very curious. "What do you see when you look at me?" I asked eagerly. "And when you looked at Ariel?"

Sally laughed. "Oh, I see a barn owl. You and Ariel and her sister are all barn owls. Barn owls, you know, have heart shaped faces. Those of the Barn Owl tribe like a close connection between the heart and the head."

I blinked my eyes rapidly. I'm not sure why, but I thought this news was going to make me cry. I sniffed and swallowed hard. But then I realized something. "You know," I said to Sally, "that feels very right right now. But I've only recently developed an affinity for the barn owl. How come it's taken me so long to recognize my own tribe?"

"Oh, no dear, your signature doesn't change, but the form I see may change--because Mariah is changing! The person you are in this incarnation may present different images to me-- and to others over the course of your incarnation--do you see? It's a way of intuitively communicating with those of your own tribe."

"Are we members of the same tribe, Sally?"

"Oh, of course, dear. We are all of us here at this table members of the same tribe. That's why you were led here to us."

They sat silently nodding, satisfied that they had led me to this most important of revelations.

"How do you see energy signatures, Al?" I asked.

He raised his eyebrows at me. "For me, it's all intuition. I just know."

Sally and Tim nodded sagely at Al's comment. They seemed in awe of this ability.

I sat silently contemplating all they'd said. I picked up my cup to sip the coffee. "That coffee is cold by now," Al said in a scolding tone. "Let's get you a warm up."

"Oh, no," I insisted. "I don't usually drink much coffee. I don't need any more or I'll be all jittery."

"Yeah," he said, "but you do want another pastry. Roger!" he called. "Bring Mariah one of those chocolate bars." I sat in awe. I had been thinking about the chocolate bars. I pulled my wallet out of my pocket as Roger brought over the pastry. "Now you put that away, Mariah. Roger'll put it on our tab." Roger nodded and went back to his post by the cash register. "Tim'll pay for it!" Al said slyly, and the three of them burst into laughter yet again.

I took a bite of my chocolate bar as Sally pushed the Chinese checkerboard into the center of the table. "You be yellow, Mariah," Al said to me.

"Gosh," I said. "I haven't played Chinese checkers since I was little. I don't think I remember how."

"It's not brain surgery," Al said. "You'll figure it out."

"Just don't let Al talk you into any wagers," Tim warned.

"You'll be fine."

We sat in silence as each of us took a few moves. "Can I ask a question?" I asked.

"About the game or about the universe?" Al asked.

"Um," I said a bit befuddled. "Well, it's not about the game."

Al rolled his eyes. "She's trying to get us off our game. And she claimed she didn't know how to play!"

"You're a shrewd one, Mariah Easter," Sally said with a laugh, but Al didn't look pleased.

"Go ahead, Mariah," Tim said. "What's your question?"

"I guess I wanted to know if you talked about all this energy stuff with Ariel? Did she understand all these things you're telling me?"

"Now that's two very different questions!" Al exclaimed, staring at the board.

Tim and Sally looked at me sympathetically. "Al's right," Sally said with a nod. "Did we talk to Ariel about these things: no. Did she understand: yes."

"We often saw Ariel and her family here at the donut shop," Tim said. "They were drawn here by our energy. But to those on the physical planes, it appeared we did nothing more than exchange pleasantries. In reality, we were doing important energetic work with Ariel and her sister Caitlin in multi-dimensional space. Ariel's higher self understood what she came here to do. In the physical realm Ariel looked like a scared little girl. But her vehicle housed a greatly advanced being."

"Your journey is somewhat different," Sally continued. "Mariah needs to be reminded of the knowledge her higher self already knows. That's why you came here."

"Okay," I said, my mind still working.

"Okay!" Al repeated. "Can we get on with it now? It's your move, Mariah!"

"Oh." I looked hard at the board and made a hasty move.

"Thank you!" Al said, his voice dripping with sarcasm. I watched as he moved his token to jump over four of ours, advancing his first piece to the other side of the board. He smiled smugly and nodded in my direction. "Thank you very much," he said, this time sounding sincere. I rested my chin in my hands, feeling glum but amused.

The game progressed, blue, green, red, and yellow marbles mingling on the wooden board. I wasn't doing too badly, but I was definitely coming in last. We spoke little throughout the game, soft requests to pass the coffee or sugar, eager boasting and teasing. I said nothing, I only watched the marbles, felt in fact that I was nearly hypnotized by their movements. They were like swarming insects, or marching band members dressed in colorful uniforms strutting across the football field at half time. I tilted my head, blinking my eyes, afraid I might fall asleep, then heard Al's voice: "It's not about seeing in the dark."

I sat up quickly. "What?" I asked turning abruptly to face Al.

The trio of elders, all bent over the board, lifted their heads slowly to gaze at me. "mmmm?" Al murmured.

"You said something," I told him. "I heard you."

"No, I didn't say anything," he told me both seriously and patiently. "But I don't doubt you heard me."

I sat back in my chair. "Bet you need more coffee now, huh?" Tim asked.

I stared at him as if he'd offered me more magic mushrooms. "It's okay," Sally assured me. "You can trust your heart."

"This really is just coffee," Tim said with a wry smile. I lifted my cup. He filled it and I then took another sip.

Al gently tapped my arm. "Your move."

I took a deep breath and focused on the board. "Oh!" I hadn't noticed this particular move before. I reached forward and rapidly moved my token across the board, jumping back and forth over Al's, Sally's and Tim's marbles. "Hey, I'm finally getting this, maybe."

Al surprised me. "Atta girl," he said softly. Tim and Sally nodded their agreement. The game went on.

Four moves later I bent over the board, amazed that the marbles made beautiful geometric patterns, resembling solar systems and constellations. I heard Al's voice again: "You're not looking into the dark; you're looking into the next dimension. You can see it, now slip inside."

I jerked my head up and stared at Al. He had his chin in his hand, watching the board. He turned to look at me. "Trust," he said.

"So are you saying--" I began, seeking clarification.

"After the game," he told me.

We played on. I felt like I'd been there for days and days, and yet the sun had yet to rise. Tim seemed to be pulling ahead, then Sally caught up with him. Al was apparently the undisputed champ, suddenly overtaking them both. But then I was suddenly capable of blocking their moves. I was amazed to realize I was in the lead. I only had one more marble to bring home. "You're vibrating faster," I heard Al say, though I knew he hadn't moved his lips. "Anything is possible."

I glared at him. "Are you trying to psych me out?" I accused.

He burst out laughing--we all did. "Celebrate with me, Mariah!" Al proclaimed as he lifted his coffee mug to clink it against the edge of mine. "You are here with us at last. You have arrived."

I smiled, still amused by my own joke, but a bit confused. What did he mean—I'd arrived at last? A metaphor or euphemism? Obviously I'd arrived here hours ago. In fact I was here before they were this morning. I was about to ask him to explain when I noticed quite suddenly the change in their physical appearances. Al and Tim each had full heads of hair, Sally's hair was long, sleek and shiny. They were each thin and fit, with flawless skin and clear eyes. None of them wore reading glasses. They were young and emitting yellow light, like halos.

They sat quietly before me, undoubtedly aware of what I was seeing. They waited as I took it all in, as I stared, my mouth gaping, my hands pressed to my cheeks in awe. Then I heard a voice calling behind me. I turned around and nearly fell off my chair. At the corner table sat Ariel: her fair skin flawless and glowing with a delicate rosy hue, her long hair spread across her narrow shoulders like a cape of sunbeams, healthy and beautiful.

I whipped back around, feeling stricken by what I had seen. "What's happening?" I breathed in fear.

Al grasped my hand. "Trust it," he said kindly. "She's here."

"Ariel," another voice chimed in. I looked up to see a smiling man with sandy colored hair receiving a pink box of pastries at the counter. "Let's go, kiddo," he called to his daughter and Ariel appeared at his side. I noticed another girl then, Ariel's twin, the same size, build, and healthy complexion standing beside them.

"See you tomorrow," Ariel cheerfully proclaimed to our table. Sally, Tim and Al waved and wished her and her family a good day. They strolled out the door in a wave of fuchsia light.

My three companions turned to me with smiling lips but concerned eyes. "It's a little disorienting at first, isn't it?" Sally said gently.

"I don't understand," I said. "Am I asleep?"

"No," Al said, "You're finally waking up."

"You're in the fifth dimension now," Tim told me. "You've been looking into this dimension for over a month, but just now--as you helped us work the harmonic patterns on the checker board--you were able to step into this space. You're with us now, here where the vibrational qualities are faster and consequently more enhanced."

"But Ariel!" I blurted. "You told me she was dead. I read her obituary."

Al laughed, but his laughter no longer had the derisive quality of an elderly curmudgeon. "Mariah!" he said in his vibrant younger voice, "you know there's no such thing as death. Ariel didn't die, she passed. If you think for a minute, you'll remember that's what we said."

I paused for a moment, and nodded. That was the term they had used, but I thought they were being euphemistic.

"She dropped her body and she placed her consciousness here in this dimension," Tim explained. "In this space there's been no need for Ariel or Caitlin to drop their bodies because they never developed melanoma. And they never developed melanoma because they vibrate too fast for the UV rays of the sun to harm them. They still have the genetic disorder that caused their disease in the lower dimension, but it's not an issue here."

"In the same way," Sally continued Tim's explanation, "we appear to be younger because we are vibrating at a much faster rate. Hence we age more slowly. Do you understand?"

"I'm not sure," I admitted. "It all sounds good and reasonably, but it's hard to fathom that this isn't a dream. But I guess it's real."

"Oh, no, Mariah," Al said as if in warning. "Don't believe that this is real." He laughed again. "None of this is real."

"There is only one reality," Sally said, "and that is God. God is the only reality, God is all. All of this--" she waved her hand to indicate the donut shop, "this is a projection we humans have agreed upon. We can manipulate it to fit our needs, but it's not real."

"We like to say that God is having a dream," Tim said, "that she's become seven billion individuals on Planet Earth. But it's only a dream."

I nodded. "My godfather likes to say that too," I told them.

"That's right," Al said. "I almost forgot. Now you tell Craig he owes us another game of Chinese checkers. It's been too long."

I nodded at this latest revelation. Of course they knew Craig. That made perfect sense. At that moment I was thinking that there was nothing more that could surprise me, but of course I was still naive about that.

I looked out the plate glass window. With my shadow busting vision, I had no idea if it was day or night outside. And I felt so disoriented, I wasn't sure if I'd been here an hour or a year. I wasn't sure what to do. There was a part of me that wanted to stay in this chair, glued to this window, eating donuts and playing checkers for the rest of my days. It felt safe, though not exactly familiar.

The shop had changed as well as the people. The place was bigger and the ceilings were higher. The table was unstained and shiny, and the chairs had thick new pads on the seats. The walls had transformed from graying white to sunny yellow. Even Roger looked more cheerful and alive. He wore no glasses, his muscles looked sculpted and lean. The fifth dimension had been good to him and his shop.

I looked down at my own body, wondering if I had changed, but I saw no sign of it. "It's true," Sally said, "you look pretty much the same."

"But don't be disappointed," Tim interjected. "You'll see lots of other changes out there."

The three of them looked at me, and I could sense a finality in their comments, a preparing for dismissal. I gripped the edge of the table, ready to beg them to let me stay. "We're here every morning," Sally said lightly. "You know where to find us."

I glanced at the board, still set before us on the table. "We didn't finish the game," I said, a bit mischievously. "I was about to win."

Al gave me an indulgent look. "You don't know what you're up against, Mariah. My advice is quit while you're ahead." I looked at him suspiciously, but something told me to let it go. The pattern was set where it needed to be. "Okay," I said.

I pushed back my chair and rose slowly. I looked toward the door, then back again. "But what if--"

Sally interrupted me. "You will encounter more than a few surprises," she told me. "But none of it will be completely unfamiliar."

"You didn't land in Oz or Neverland," Tim said. "You're still here in Sacramento. It's not different, just enhanced."

Al burst out laughing. "Mariah! We're with you, you know that. You can hear me even when I'm not talking. Well, guess what, I can hear you too. What have you got to worry about?"

"Okay," I said. I ventured into the center of the shop, and wavered at the counter, tempted to buy another donut for the road. "You're not even hungry!" I heard Al's voice. "Stop distracting yourself!"

I turned back toward him, but he had not spoken aloud. I looked at him in an accusatory way. "If you didn't want to hear it," he said while moving his lips, "you wouldn't hear it." I rolled my eyes and headed for the door. One hand on the knob, I turned and lifted my other hand in an abbreviated wave. Sally, Tim and Al were woven together in an intricate Celtic knot of colorful lights. They called their farewells, but my eyes stung from the intensity of their brilliance. Blinking and nodding, I slipped out the door.

Chapter Twenty-Five
Mariah

I stood on the sidewalk, wondering if it were day or night. I glanced at my cell phone and it was nearing 12, but I honestly wouldn't have been surprised to discover it was midnight instead of noon. I looked up Broadway and heard myself gasp. The street was neat and well kept. The restaurants and shops were shaded with dark blue and green awnings, giving the district a refined air. The sidewalks were lined by gardens and fresh green grass. New Canton and Los Jarritos boasted fresh herbs out front, as well as statues of their favored goddesses: Kuan Yin by New Canton, the Black Madonna of Guadalupe by Los Jarritos. I was elated to see their influence.

The adult bookstore and video shop were gone, replaced with a new locally owned place that claimed to specialize in maps, atlases, geography and travel books. I wondered how a shop with such a narrow focus could make it in today's market, but then I saw how crowded the shop was with people browsing, sipping coffee, and making purchases. A children's bookshop was next door, and the greasy auto body shop had been replaced by a Toyota show room. What a surprise to see a car dealership on this lonely street, I thought, but another glance showed me the street was lonely no more. People were everywhere, some dressed in business suits, others in khakis and jackets. It struck me that there was no one who appeared to be homeless or destitute, no one down on his luck. Well, this neighborhood has been gentrified, I thought. I guess they've moved elsewhere.

I had been wondering where I should go. Should I go home? Rafa would be at school, so there was no great urgency to go to our flat. Should I go to school? Truth be told, I'd already missed two morning classes, so unless I needed to hang in the library, there was no necessity to go there either. Now the energy had led me to pose this question: where had the poor gone, the street people who often wandered Broadway begging for spare change or a chance to wash your windshield for a dollar or two--what neighborhood were they haunting now? I turned down 26th and headed north. I would go to our church. Noon mass would be starting soon, and perhaps I'd have the courage to ask our pastor what life was like for the poor in the fifth dimension.

I hiked the fourteen blocks over to St. Francis Church across from Sutter's Fort. It was a cold and sunny day, the light so bright it made every object, every car, tree, flower and lamp post look crisp and radiant. The urban landscape looked as if it had been painted in a single light coat of glittering watercolor. Everything looked wet and glossy, not pressed with a heavy velvety brush, but rather with a watery sheen, pastels as fresh as butter mint candles.

The hundred-year-old church towered above the street like a sheltering mountain. I liked coming here. I felt secure here. The bell was ringing as I climbed the steps.

I hastened inside. There was only a handful of people there to attend a mid-week mid-day mass. The congregants were singing a hymn I hadn't heard in a while "Christ, be our light: shine in our hearts, shine in the darkness." I felt moved listening to the lyrics, hoping this could be manifest in me now, in this strange new dimension. The celebrant had already entered by the center aisle before I had arrived. He stood below the altar, joining in the hymn, his back to the gathered assemblage. I looked at the back of his head, and realized that he looked unfamiliar. Perhaps a new priest was visiting from out of town. Franciscans often came from the Bay Area or from their Provincial headquarters in Santa Barbara. I wasn't surprised to see a stranger, and it didn't occur to me right away that this new priest might have been due to the change in dimensions.

As we sang the last verse of the hymn, I watched as the priest mounted the steps. He walked around the center table and bowed to kiss it. My heart leapt into my throat. It was the brown haired homeless man whom I had first seen a month ago sleeping on the church steps. It was he who had helped the other woman and I escape through the kitchen of that awful dance club. He was the one I had seen sleeping beneath the freeway just this morning. I squinted at him as he began the opening prayers. How could this be possible? I remembered then my question, why the energy had led me there: where had the poor gone? But here in this church, here was one man, once homeless, now welcomed as Christ's celebrant.

We sat for the daily readings. A woman I saw sometimes at mass, but whom I did not know, took her place at the side microphone to read a passage from the psalms. I could barely attend to her recitation. I looked around in curiosity, wondering what changes I might note here. The lights seemed a little brighter, the people looked a little better dressed than usual, but other than that all seemed the same. I mulled this over, curious, but accepting of the scenario presented to me. My head snapped forward. All were standing for the reading of the gospel.

The new priest stood at the podium, coincidentally reading one of my favorite quotes: *I am the way, the truth and the life; all who believe in me, shall not die but be born to eternal life.* His voice had a mellow quality to it, like an Andean panpipe, deep and woody. He had a slight accent, and I remembered that his few words to us had been Spanglish, freely mixing both languages. I also remembered with affection how he had called us "mijas," *my daughters.* Even in the panic of our frantic escape, it had warmed my heart to be addressed with such familial concern.

We stood for the consecration, and as so often happens I found my mind drifting even at this most sacred of moments. I berated myself to pay attention, to listen for those most magic and mystical of words, "This is my body, this is my blood." As a

Christian, I was raised to believe there was nothing more important, and how honored I was to live in a city named for this most sacred of Divine gifts. When the priest came down to serve us, I got in line with everyone else. I bowed, as I have been taught to do, before I approached and with outstretched palms waited for him to say the sacred words.

"Body of Christ, Mariah," he said with a welcoming smile. I was so shocked that he knew my name, I could barely remember the simple response. I stood frozen for an instant. "Mariah?" he prompted, and I quickly blurted, "Amen." He put the host into my hand and I placed it reverentially in my mouth.

I went to the pew and sank onto my knees. Tim had told me I would encounter surprises. The beautiful gardens and bustling new shops on Broadway had certainly been different, but as surprises go, they were nothing compared to this. Did I dare speak to this man after mass? Could I pretend to know him, would I be able to carry it off? And how would I ever be able to ask him about the homeless that we serve here at this church, when he himself was so recently one of the many welcomed onto the sanctuary of these steps? I remembered I had just received the Eucharist. Nothing could touch me, nothing could harm me now that I was here safe in this church, in the embrace of the Divine Oneness that was the Eucharist. If I appeared confused or embarrassed myself with naive questions when speaking to this priest, what did it matter?

The priest moved out to the front steps to greet the departing congregants. I followed along, hanging back, waiting for the words that might guide me. Still uninspired, I watched as others exchanged quick pleasantries with him and then descended the steps. He turned to me, and I had no choice but to move forward. "Mariah!" he exclaimed, wrapping his arm around me paternalistically. "What a wonderful surprise to see you at midday mass! How is my beautiful daughter-in-law today?"

I pulled back in shock, or maybe I nearly fell over; I'll never know for sure. "What?" I blurted quickly, all hope of appearing casual and sane gone.

"I said, 'how are you?' Are you okay?"

I nodded vigorously. "Yes," I said emphatically. "I'm fine. And you? How are you?"

"Bueno! What a beautiful day, no?"

"Yes, beautiful," I repeated. "The air is so clean, you know, after the rain."

"Yes, mija, and what brings you here today at noon? Are you praying for a special intention?"

I thought, jeez louise, can't you tell I'm praying that you'll tell me why you called me daughter-in-law! But of course I couldn't say that. Or could I? It would be strange, but maybe I should confess that I'd fallen out of a completely different dimension, and I was having a little trouble navigating the landscape here. Could you recommend a guide? I took a deep breath. "I have many prayer intentions," I revealed coyly. "But I can't say yet. You know, it's kind of a secret."

He laughed. "Oh, I see. Okay. Well, maybe I can get the secret out of Rafa. My son is not so good at keeping secrets."

My jaw fell into my chest. "Your son!" I exclaimed. "Rafa is your son?"

He gave me a very odd look. I held my breath. Now I was in trouble. Obviously I was supposed to know that this man was Rafa's father, and my ignorance of that fact had revealed me to be a fraud. I swallowed hard, breathing shallowly, wondering what to say, when suddenly he burst out laughing. "Okay, okay, I will leave your secrets alone; I won't go pestering Rafa to find out what they are. I'm sure you'll tell me when the time is right." He shook his head, still chuckling, obviously marveling about how funny I was. An idea came to me.

"So," I ventured in a purposely fake and playful tone, "tell me more about this Rafa. So he's a friend of mine you say? And he also happens to be your son?"

"That's right, you silly girl. Your husband, Rafa—he's my son!" He laughed heartily again. "I've got to get to a meeting, mija. Tell your mom I'm looking forward to dinner at her house this week!" He bent and kissed my cheek. "Adios, mija!"

He took the church steps at a spry clip and headed toward the rectory. I stood stunned. This was Rafa's father? And Rafa and I were married? I leaned on a pillar, feeling a bit weak. This was crazy. How could any of this be possible? There was a sound behind me, as the church custodian began to pull the front door closed. "Oh, wait," I said quickly. "Are there any bulletins left from last weekend?" I asked.

"Sure," he acknowledged. "There are a few on this table." He motioned me into the vestibule and fetched me the bulletin. "Thank you," I said and I darted across the street to the park surrounding the fort.

Once there I stood on the wet grass and leafed through the bulletin. In the fifth dimension the parish saw fit to publish an eight-page weekly newsletter with contemplations on Biblical passages and features on volunteers of the week. Impressive.

In the back they listed the church staff, same as they did back in my original dimension. There was an associate pastor whose name I did not recognize: Ignacio Salvador. This must be my mysterious father-in-law. I sighed, looking around me, afraid I would be seen and recognized. After all, it was a good bet that I was well known. How many Catholic priests would have sons and daughters-in-law?

My next logical move might be to go home and google Father Ignacio. But I wasn't ready to go home and face a Rafa whom I was apparently married to. I could go to the school library and use the computers there. I rocked on my feet and suddenly realized that my heart was racing. Time to slow down and think. I sank onto the damp grass, naturally folding my legs into a modified lotus positon. Think! I told myself, then Al's voice told me, *No! Don't think. TRUST.* I closed my eyes, breathed deeply and began to silently chant. "Lord, Jesus Christ, they kingdom come..."

Oh wow, maybe that's what this was--the kingdom had come! No, no, don't think. I began chanting again.

My father's face floated into my head. Hey, if Ariel was still alive...

Would that even be possible? I knew now where I wanted to go. I stood and started walking to our old house in midtown.

As I walked I imagined what it would be like to see my father again after nearly three years without him. In this dimension he would be healthy and disease free, and he and Mom would be happily retired, traveling and gardening, arguing and laughing. And what would it be like to be married to Rafa? That would be weird. I mean we considered ourselves siblings. I could no more marry him than I could marry Dale. That would just be too strange. Or would it? We certainly have an amazing rapport. I get along with Rafa better than I have with any other man. We laugh together and tease each other, the same way my mom and dad always did. And Rafa is certainly sexy enough. It's not that looks are that important, but the fact he was cute was a nice bonus. But could Rafa settle down? He really seemed to run through women quick. Would he be loyal to me? When I considered myself his sister, I didn't mind his flirtatious nature. But now that we were married--wow, I made that leap in my mind fast. Sure, but the idea was still pretty weird.

I rounded the corner and saw the house where I grew up. Mom hadn't sold it when she bought the new house; she decided to rent it. I think she couldn't let go of it yet. But if Daddy were still alive, I'm thinking then Mom wouldn't have gotten the money from his life insurance, and they'd still be living here. But what if they weren't? Just then a tall muscular man came sprinting out of the craftsman mansion next door. "Mariah!" he called as he headed for a white pick-up truck. "Whatcha doing in the old neighborhood?"

I had to do a double take. It was Hal, a man who'd been our neighbor for a decade or more. But in my previous dimension Hal weighed upwards of 300 pounds and he waddled. Here he is fit and he sprints from the door to his car. Amazing. But more curious: is he calling this the "old neighborhood" because Mom has moved near the American River, or because I've moved north in midtown? I held my breath, wondering how to extract information without tipping my hand. "Just out for a walk," I said meekly, raising my eyebrows and giving him a simpering smile, hoping he'd fill in the rest. But he stood there, nodding and grinning, and certainly not holding up his end of the conversation. "How've you been?" I finally said in a leisurely and amiable tone, tilting my head and gesturing with my hands as if I wanted nothing more than to chat all day.

"Great," he said. "And yourself? And your mom? How's your mom? We sure do miss her here. How's she liking that new place in River Park?"

My heart sank, and I hoped I wouldn't cry. Daddy must be dead. Still dead, that is. What was I all broken up about, jeez. "Mom is fine," I managed with a smile. "She's doing great."

"You tell her I said hello," he instructed as he pulled open his car door.

I nodded and waved and hastened by my beloved house. I rounded the corner quickly. I had no doubt where I was going now. I wanted to see my mom.

I hiked two blocks down and eight blocks over to the flat I

shared with Rafa. As I approached I wondered if we still lived here; maybe as a young married couple we'd settled somewhere else. I heard there was subsidized housing for married students on the far end of campus. What if we lived there? But I was relieved to see my car still parked in front of the flat, where I'd left it this morning. Rafa's car was in front of mine, but I still wasn't ready to encounter him, now that I was Mrs. Rafa and he was Mr. Mariah. I ran over to my car, unlocked it and stashed my backpack inside. With furtive glances to our upstairs apartment, I got inside and closed the door as quietly as possible. I started up the engine and headed to River Park.

I pulled into my mother's driveway and entered the house through the garage as I always did. As I opened the door, it occurred to me that not only was this the fifth dimension, it was also the middle of the week. My mother would not be expecting me, so I should be careful not to startle her. "Mom!" I called in a loud voice. There was no immediate response so I headed down the hall. Gosh, what if she'd bought some other house in the fifth dimension? There was no telling what I might encounter next. "Mom!" I yelled again.

"Mariah?" she answered, coming out of her bedroom. "What are you doing here?"

I stopped dead in my tracks and stared at her. She looked younger than I had ever seen her, in fact she didn't look much older than I am. Her shorn hair was long again, thick and shiny. I was stunned because I'd always thought my Mom was attractive, but now her face seemed to glow. Her skin looked dewy and her eyelashes were dark and thick. She wore a tank top and her arms and shoulders were softly sculpted as if she'd been lifting weights. I was dumb-struck.

Seeing me frozen like this, she stopped too. "What's the matter?" she blurted, rattling off a chain of questions. "Is something wrong? Why are you here in the middle of the day?"

I shook my head to wake myself. "Everything is fine!" I assured her with exaggerated cheeriness. "I was, um--class! That's it, my class got canceled, so I thought I'd come on over-- you know, since I was in the neighborhood and all." I paused, then had a sudden idea. "I know! Maybe we can go out to lunch. That would be something that we normally do on occasion, right?"

"I'm sorry, sweetie," she said, as she led me back to the living room. "I've already eaten lunch. It's nearly 1:30! I can fix you a sandwich. How bout grilled cheese?"

"Okay," I said, because when your mom offers you comfort food like grilled cheese you always say yes.

We moved into the kitchen and I seated myself on a bar stool round the work island as she pulled French bread from the pantry and cheese from the fridge. "Swiss or cheddar?" she asked. I could always depend on Mom to have many options. I don't think she was used to cooking for one yet. "Cheddar," I told her, feeling grateful that she was the same regardless of her youthful appearance.

"What class got canceled?" she asked as she got out a frying pan and buttered the bread.

"Oh, um, calculus," I told her, stretching the truth since that was the class I'd inadvertently missed that morning. "Yeah, it would have been calculus this morning. Yeah, that's a bad one to miss. But you know, the professor canceled on us. So that's okay. In a case like that I didn't miss anything." God, I sounded drunk!

I looked around the room. Everything looked much as it had the last time I was there. A framed photo of my parents caught my eye. They both looked young in this picture, standing in a field of flowers at Daffodil Hill. I'd taken that picture five or six years ago, and they hadn't looked that young in my dimension. How could my father have died when he looked so young and healthy?

"Whatcha up to, Mom?" I asked. "Am I keeping you from anything?"

"Nothing I can't do later, you know," she said as she placed the sandwich in the pan. "Still trying to decide what to take with me to India."

"India?" I exclaimed. Okay, I thought, I can handle this. Don't act so surprised. So she's taking a trip to India. "India," I repeated in a more controlled voice. She had never expressed any desire to travel to India, I thought. Why India? "Tell me again when you leave?" I asked, trying to sound casual.

She rolled her eyes. "Mariah, Mariah!" she exclaimed with a laugh. "I guess I should be happy that you're so focused on midterms. I hope you and Rafa don't forget to drive me to San Francisco on Saturday."

"I'm sorry! You know it's on my big calendar in the kitchen. I won't forget."

"I'm sorry too," she said. "I know it's not the best time to take off for the city, the Saturday after Thanksgiving. I'm sure there'll be lots of traffic. But I have no control over the retreat schedule. It is what it is!" She flipped the sandwich with a wooden spatula.

"Right," I nodded, trying to keep up. "The retreat schedule." I tried to give my voice a leading tone. Maybe she would see that as an opening, and jump in with more information.

"It's going to be so interesting, getting to study at the ashram," she gushed. "After that, I'll only need one more class, and then I'll have my instructor's certification. But what a blessing, to be able to take this class from a yoga master!"

"Instructor's certification!" I exclaimed. "For yoga? What a great idea! That'll be perfect for you."

She lifted my sandwich onto a plate. "I know," she said in a matter of fact way. Obviously I'd already gotten all excited about this for her in the past. Like the first time she told me about it. Now my belated enthusiasm seemed silly. She handed me the sandwich on a familiar ceramic plate.

"And this class," I started again, "it's going to--um, it's going to take how long?"

"Three weeks, Mariah. Are you okay? We've talked about this so many times."

"I know, Mom; I'm sorry for being forgetful." I took a bite of my sandwich. Oh my God, did all the food taste so good in this dimension? This was incredible. Now I was a little annoyed that Al had talked me out of eating another donut. Donuts must be magnificent in this dimension.

"I'm going to make it back in time for Christmas," she said as she seated herself across from me at the island. "I don't know how many times I have to tell you that."

"Well, it wouldn't be Christmas without you," I said congenially. "This sandwich is really good, Mom. Thank you." She leaned forward and we gave each other a hug and a kiss. Thank God some things hadn't changed.

"Mariah," she said as I continued eating. "I happened to see some really nice garnet yams at the farmer's market yesterday, so I picked them up for the pies. You should go ahead and take them."

"Pies," I said tentatively.

"Did you buy the pecans?" she asked.

"Pecans," I said, realizing that this one called for a response. "Not yet," I ventured bravely.

"I didn't see any at the market, so you'll just have to get them at the grocery store. I should have gotten you some while

I was shopping yesterday. If I were you I'd go get what you need today. The stores will be so busy tomorrow."

I nearly choked on my sandwich as I realized what she was saying. She said she was leaving this Saturday, didn't she? And she said that Saturday was the weekend after Thanksgiving! So this Thursday. But it was only a few days past Halloween this morning when I went to the donut shop! This couldn't be possible!

"Thanksgiving really snuck up on me this year!" I proclaimed.

"Well, it's pretty darn early that's for sure," Mom agreed.

"Who all is coming for dinner?" I asked casually.

Again she rolled her eyes. "Who do you think?" she asked sarcastically. "Do you think I asked the cast of the play I saw last night at the B Street Theater? Just family: Dale and Luisa, Anna, and you and Rafa, and of course Father Ignacio." That's right, Father Ignacio had told me to tell Mom he was looking forward to dinner at her house. Okay, that explained that.

"Ignacio is such a nice man," she said suddenly. I sat up straighter. Did I detect a girlish gleam in that remark? "You know he gave me his email address. He said to be sure to write to him while I'm in India."

I stared at her. She seemed absolutely giddy when she spoke about this man. But the guy was a priest! How he happened to be a priest and Rafa's father was still a bit beyond me. I wondered if I might be able to get around to that in the conversation, but Mom was leaning toward me in a conspiratorial way.

"Mariah," she said slowly. "I need to tell somebody this. No, I really need to tell *you* this." She sat up again and swallowed, as if she had bad news.

"What's the matter?" I asked, concerned.

"Nothing," she said quickly. "Nothing is wrong. Maybe something is finally right." She blinked back a few tears, then pushed her hair away from her face. "Mariah, I never thought I'd be interested in having another relationship with a man after your father died, but Father Ignacio seems interested, and I have to admit, I'm thinking about it. I hope that doesn't upset you."

"Mom!" I blurted. "He's a priest!"

She sat back and stared at me as if shocked. "What does that matter?" she said. "Of course being the companion of a pastor wouldn't be easy, and you're right, that could be particularly difficult for me, since I'm such an introvert, but-- well, I'm just thinking of dating right now, let's not jump way ahead."

I sat there with my mouth open, half the uneaten sandwich in my right hand. "But, Mom," I began trying to wrap my mind around this, "I mean, he's a priest. You can't marry a priest-- can you?" I felt lost and stupid suddenly.

She laughed. "Right," she said, "certainly there will be those who will be prejudiced, who think we need to go back to those Pre-Vatican II days when priests couldn't get married. Now that kind of thing I can handle. And so can you. Don't think you won't encounter that kind of bigotry when you're ordained."

"What?" Maybe I didn't hear her right. Obviously I didn't hear her right.

"When you finish your training and you're ordained," she said again in a matter of fact way, "you and Rafa will encounter some bigotry. It's inevitable. Not only a woman, but a married woman. No matter. When you have a vocation--"

She paused to stare at me. I was slumped in my seat,

trying to swallow this last mouthful that suddenly seemed very dry. I was going to be a priest? That was outrageous. I didn't want to be a priest. I wanted to be a social worker or a teacher like my mom was. A priest? That had never occurred to me. But then why would it? It hadn't been allowed, so I had never considered it. If it had been acceptable, and in this dimension it was, well, maybe I would have given the idea more than a passing thought.

Well, obviously I had.

"Are you all right?" Mom asked me. "Can I get you something to drink?"

"Some water would be nice," I told her. She gave me a glass and I drank it slowly.

"Mom," I said. "Would you mind if I took the rest of my sandwich to go? I just remembered a few errands I should go run."

"That's fine, sweetie. Let me get you those yams."

"I'm making a sweet potato pie for Thanksgiving?" I asked her.

"You told me you found a recipe on line that you liked. With pecan topping? Did I get that wrong? Of course, you can make any kind of pie that you like, Mariah."

"Okay," I said. "It's just that Anna usually brings the pies, doesn't she? You know, from her shop--"

"Anna sold the pie shop chain five years ago, Mariah," Mom said. "You know all she does is chair the charitable foundation now."

"Right," I said nodding, surprised again and trying to recover. "Still making a pie for the great Anna Victoria, pie-maker extraordinaire!-- it can be a little intimidating, you know."

Mom laughed. "Oh, Mariah, I don't think Anna has even gone into a kitchen herself for decades!" She shook her head. "You know she was trying again last week to get me to join the board of directors of her foundation. I told her, no, thank you, ma'am. I am much happier working on a small scale!"

"Good decision," I said feeling it was safe to agree.

She handed me a cloth tote bag filled with yams and I traveled off, circling the block slowly, wondering if I was ready to meet my husband. It seemed I had nowhere left to go.

Chapter Twenty-Six
Mariah

I parked in front of our flat and slowly mounted the stairs. I wasn't sure what I would say to Rafa, but if I couldn't tell him my secret--well, then there was no one I would ever be able to trust again. I tried the knob. The door was open.

"Hey, Babe," Rafa called from the kitchen. "Where've you been all day?" He appeared in the doorway to the dining room, looking just like himself, the exact same Rafa whom I love like a brother. But now he was my husband: how was that going to work? I always knew he was good-looking, and well sexy too, but still, it worried me.

"I've had a crazy day," I said with a forced smile, and then he was across the room, taking me in his arms. It was overwhelming but nice. He smelled good: I wondered what he'd been cooking? His hands were in my hair. Oh my God, this was different. I pulled away.

"Tell me about your crazy day," he said as he headed back into the kitchen. "You left awfully early. I didn't even hear you go."

I wanted to blurt out that he didn't hear me go because I'd been sleeping in a different bed in a different room. But I just smiled. "I went for an early morning walk," I said. This was honest. So far so good.

"Why, Babe? Couldn't you sleep? Is something bothering you?" He picked up a wooden spatula and pushed at chopped onions he had frying in a pan. Same old Rafa with the frying pan. He dumped a plate of sliced mushrooms in there too. "You okay?" he asked.

"Oh, yeah," I said. But he continued to stare at me. "No," I said finally. "It's not that there's anything wrong, not really. It's just that I'm having trouble today, you know, keeping up with everything."

"In school?" he asked. "What are you worried about? You're acing that calculus class. Is it a different one?"

"No, it's not school." I paused. "It's just that--what are you doing?" He was removing the onions and mushrooms from the pan and blotting them with a paper towel.

"What?" he asked, seemingly confused, as if he were doing nothing unusual. "I'm removing some of the fat." He slid the cleaner, healthier veggies into a bigger pot and added some chopped tomatoes he'd had in a bowl I hadn't noticed.

"What are you making?" I asked.

"The usual spaghetti sauce," he said. "This is your recipe, the one you created. Why are you standing there with your mouth open like you've forgotten how to cook?" He laughed and grabbed me playfully, tickling my ribs and kissing my cheek. I was startled and amazed, torn between hugging him back and pulling away. I wanted to hug him back, but who knew where that might lead? He was kissing my neck now, and it appeared he might head south any moment. I pushed him back gently. "Rafa," I said. "I need to talk to you."

I leaned past him and turned off the gas burner. "Can we sit down?"

He shrugged. "Sure," he said, unconcerned. We went into the dining room.

"I'm not sure how to talk about this," I began as we both settled into our usual chairs. He bent his head like an alert dog listening for a sound we humans can't detect. "This morning I was a different person," I told him.

"Wow," he said. "Some life altering event happened to you today?" He was obviously sincere and curious, and I realized this was one of the reasons why I loved him. He would never make fun of me, or even tease me about something I was still trying to figure out. He had a kindness that was very rare for a young man.

"You know," I said, "that is it exactly. This morning I went for a walk down to this donut shop on Broadway, and I met three people there. Three very wise people--and you know what--they happen to be friends with Craig."

His eyebrows shot up. "Are they perfect masters like Craig?"

"Perfect--?" I paused. I'd never heard Craig called a perfect master before, and I wasn't sure what that meant. I was curious, but I felt my situation warranted urgency so I forged on. "Um, I really don't know what they are, but there were three of them--Al, Tim and Sally. Tim and Sally were very sweet. Al was kind of grouchy, though he was definitely the most advanced and very helpful in his way."

"What did they tell you?" Rafa asked in a hushed tone.

I leaned across the table and touched his hand. "They told me that I had been looking into a different dimension, and that the time had come for me to actually enter that dimension."

Rafa sat back scowling. "I don't know if I like that idea, Mariah. That could be dangerous without the right support. I think you should run this by Craig. And I don't want you trying it unless I'm there to spot you."

"Rafa," I said slowly. "I already did it. I didn't even know I was doing it. We played a game of Chinese checkers and when the game was done, I was here."

"Here?" he asked, his brow furrowed.

"Here! This--right here--is a different dimension than I started in this morning."

"You're kidding!" he said, laughing, leaning forward with interest. "How can you tell you're in a different dimension? Things don't look any different to me! Do they look different to you?"

"Oh, Rafa," I said sadly. "Things look so different to me. I'm so confused."

He was out of his chair and pulling me into his arms immediately. "It's okay, babe, it's okay. We're going to talk you down. Tell me what's changed?"

I pulled back again. "Rafa, so much." I pressed my lips together, unsure of what to share. But I knew it wasn't time to tell him that we weren't married where I came from. We weren't even lovers. "Could you tell me one thing, Rafa? Tell me about your mom and dad, because something has changed there, and I think it's very important."

"My mom and dad?" he repeated. "You know the story. How did it change?"

I grabbed his hand. "Please tell me the story again, Baby. I need to hear it."

"Okay," he agreed, and he led me to the couch in the living room. We sat closer than we ever had before, his arm wrapped around my shoulders, my head pressed against his chest. I had called him "Baby" a minute ago. It had just slipped out. It felt very natural.

"My parents were married in San Dismas before the junta. He was a seminarian, and she was studying to be a teacher. They met and were married, and then I was born. But there was a movement down there, a group of people who wanted to go back to the old teachings before priests could marry. They harassed my parents so much that they decided they wanted to move here to this country to raise me in peace. My father applied to come serve with the Franciscans in the Province of Santa Barbara here in California. He was accepted right away. But the week before we were to leave, one of the men who was in this reactionary movement, he saw my mother riding her bicycle home from the market. He chased her in his car, yelling at her and calling her bad names like 'slut' and 'whore,' saying she had seduced a good holy man, and she would burn in hell for it. My mother tried to ignore him and just kept riding, but then they came to a curve and there was a farmer with a truckload of pigs coming from the other direction. My mother turned wide to avoid this man who was harassing her. She didn't see the pig truck and the truck ran right into her. She was killed immediately."

"Oh Rafa," I said. "How awful."

He leaned back to look at my face. "Mariah, don't you remember this story?"

"Rafa, where I came from this morning, you had no idea who your mother or your father even were," I told him.

"Mariah, that's outrageous! I was raised by my father-- with the help of his cousin Anna. She's the one who helped my father get the work visas and citizenship applications. I've never lived apart from my father."

He pulled me close again, and I finally began to relax in his arms. "Rafa, how do you know this is what happened to your mother? Were there witnesses?"

"No," he said, "but the man who harassed her--he came forward and confessed. He felt very guilty. He admitted he had been very mean to her, that he had meant to bully her but not to kill her. He did time in prison. My understanding is that he was paroled and then he joined a cloistered monastery. He took a vow of silence, because it was his unkind words that had caused her death."

"Wow," I murmured.

"I know," Rafa replied, then he chuckled. "Well, you know," he pointed out, "in a nation named after the Good Thief, we take honesty very seriously. Penance and Reconciliation—it's the most honored of the sacraments there."

"I didn't know that," I said, feeling a bit overwhelmed. There was so much here I didn't know.

"Don't worry about it," he whispered as he massaged my scalp. I sighed, content in his arms. Then he tilted me back and gave me a long soulful kiss. I tightened my fingers on his shoulder. I wanted to, but I couldn't, not yet.

"Baby, I need to go for a walk," I told him.

"I'll go with you," he said.

"No, not yet. I need to clear my head." I kissed him lightly on the lips. "I'll be back soon." He walked me to the door. It took every ounce of strength I had to walk across the threshold.

I started walking slowly, but I picked up my pace and soon I was nearly running. I knew exactly where I needed to go: back to the donut shop. I had no idea if Al, Sally and Tim would be there. I had no idea if the shop would even be open, but I trusted that I would find my answers there. The energy was taking me; it seemed I had no choice.

Chapter Twenty-Seven
Mariah

It was still daylight. I wondered if everyone in this dimension could see in the dark, but I didn't want to stay long enough to find out.

The donut shop was like a beacon, its windows shone with yellow light. I approached it hungrily, wondering if Roger would let me sit there all night waiting for the three wise ones to show up in the morning.

I flung the door open and nearly started crying with gratitude. There they sat, just as I had left them hours earlier: Al, Sally and Tim, youthful and healthy-looking. But beside them at the table, at the seat I had occupied this morning, was Craig. He didn't look different at all. He was still the balding, 70-year-old elder who was my godfather. He wasn't playing checkers with the others, but was bent over his laptop computer, typing diligently. No one was speaking; they all appeared to be very focused at the tasks at hand.

"Craig!" I blurted joyfully at catching sight of his familiar face and he half rose to hug me. He closed his laptop, then pulled a chair up to the table for me. We both sat down again. "I've been expecting you," he told me.

"Really?" I asked.

"No," he said with a wry smile, "not really, but imaginatively."

I looked at him confused, but I ventured on. "Did they tell you I've slipped into a new dimension?" I asked him.

"No," he said briefly.

"We didn't have to tell him," Sally interjected.

"Craig just knows," Tim said.

I glanced around the table at each of them, surprised at the deferential attitude they held for my godfather. They looked expectantly at me. "You have questions," Craig said.

I stared at him for a moment. So many questions had been plaguing me all day, and yet now I was drawing a blank. My heart was racing. "You look just the same," I told Craig. "My mother looks younger here in this dimension, and so do Sally, Tim and Al. How come you look the same?"

"I am not in the fifth dimension," Craig told me. "Nor am I in the third dimension. I live interdimensionally, and I appear as I appear wherever you may encounter me."

"He's going for that 'Elder Sage' look," Al said with a laugh. Craig laughed heartily at this teasing comment, but he also gave Al a piercing stare, and Al seemed to shrink a little into his chair. I looked between the two of them, wondering what old rivalry might be in play. Sally and Tim were silent, but looked amused.

"Mariah," Craig said gently, "you've had quite an adventure here. I know you have questions."

"Maybe she needs something to eat or drink first," Tim said.

"Thank you, but I'm okay," I said, though I noticed I was breathing rapidly. "I'm just very confused. This morning I was in the third dimension where Ariel was dead, my mother was aging, priests were forbidden to marry, and Rafa was my best friend. Now I'm in a dimension where Ariel is alive and well, my mother seems to be getting younger by the minute, she's dating a priest, and I'm married to Rafa. What I don't understand is--which one of these is real?"

"Neither," Craig said emphatically.

"We told her that already," Al said, and Craig gave him a withering look.

"The only reality is God," Craig said. "What we see before us: it's a dream, a projection of Divinity exploring consciousness."

"So in the past I was dreaming that Rafa was my friend, but now I'm dreaming that Rafa is my husband?" I asked.

"Try thinking of it as exploring different potentials," Craig said. "Your vehicle has reached a level of advancement so that you may alter your perceived reality in order to expand your range of experience."

I stared at him, dumbfounded and feeling hollow. Craig smiled at me. "A chocolate donut would probably help, right? Can we get you a donut?"

"No, no," I whined. "I don't want to spoil my dinner. Rafa was cooking for me."

My voice trailed off. I didn't want to go back to that Rafa, luscious as his kisses were. I wanted to go back to my Rafa, my best friend and brother, Rafa. I looked forward to going home to him, knowing that there was indeed a vast energetic potential that might develop there, that there was a potential first kiss and a first love-making that awaited me with him, rather than going back to this Rafa who was already my husband, a Rafa that I didn't really know.

"Craig, I feel like Jimmy Stewart in *It's a Wonderful Life*, except everything I've seen here in this dimension has been great. My mother looks young and healthy, and she's happier and more hopeful about life than I've seen her since my father died. And Rafa--we have an energy together I never knew was possible. Oh, I don't know! I would be foolish to leave such a wonderful dimension, don't you think?"

Craig listened and considered the question carefully. "Only

you can decide where to place your consciousness."

"Is that all I'm doing? Placing my consciousness?"

"Exactly."

I lifted both hands to my head, feeling as if I were thinking so hard that I needed to hold my brain or I wouldn't be able to sit upright. "But what about my family in the third dimension? What happens to them if I stay here?" I asked. "And what happens to the people here if I go back to my original dimension?"

"Mariah," Craig said very slowly. "That isn't relevant because in the truest sense your family doesn't really exist. The third dimension doesn't exist. The fifth dimension doesn't exist. Mariah and Craig don't exist. Only God exists. Mariah may make the decision of where to place her consciousness completely guilt free, without regard to the feelings of others, because no one else exists."

I stood up abruptly. "That's outrageous. I can't wrap my head around that."

Craig stood up too. "Let's get you that donut," he said.

We approached the counter and waited, but Roger was nowhere to be found. "Listen," Craig said. "Think of it this way: you are never separate from those you perceive to be your family, because separateness is an illusion. We are all one, the very love that forms Divine essence." Roger appeared in the doorway that leads to the kitchen. Craig called out his order. "One chocolate old fashioned, one buttermilk bar." He turned back to the table. "You want anything?" he asked.

"A half dozen glazed for the table," Al said.

"Fine," Craig agreed, then he held out his palm. Al reluctantly pulled out his wallet and gave him a twenty. Craig shouted out to Roger and the order was brought quickly. We returned to the table and Craig gave Al the change.

"Now, Mariah," Craig continued, "each of us decides before we are born what we will experience to learn the lessons and make the spiritual advancements we want to make. But sometimes we have to take a lot of time to prepare our vehicles--our bodies--to make them able to withstand this journey. If our bodies begin to vibrate too quickly without the proper preparation, they'll lose all integrity."

"You mean we drop dead?" I asked.

He winced and nodded. "Essentially. But you see, you have been very nimble in preparing your vehicle. You've reached a point where you aren't even waiting until your next incarnation to expand your options. Do you understand?"

"I think so," I said.

He bit into his buttermilk bar, as I broke the chocolate old fashioned into bite-sized pieces. "Actually, Craig," I said. "I don't really understand anything except you got my favorite donut right. This is my favorite."

He put his arm around me. "And you want to go home," he stated in a matter of fact way.

"Yes!" I exclaimed, tears welling up in my eyes.

"Oh, Mariah," Sally said, "it was too much too soon. We're sorry."

"I'm not sorry," Al said petulantly. "She came here and we opened the door. That's all. We didn't push her through it, she went through it herself."

"Oh, no," I said, sniffling a little. "I'm not blaming anybody. In fact, I'm grateful to have had this experience, to have gotten to see what the world could be like. I want to go back to my family and tell them what I've learned. My mom would be a great yoga instructor, for example: I think that's something she might want to try. And Rafa's father--maybe I can help bring about some healing there."

"And your friend Rafa," Al said slyly, "I guess you've gotten a few ideas about how you can enhance that relationship!"

I felt myself blush, but Craig touched my shoulder. "It all happened exactly the way it needed to," he told me.

I turned to him. "You knew, didn't you? When I was telling you about how I could see in the dark. You knew I was really looking into another dimension!"

"Oh, no, Mariah," he assured me. "If I'd known I would have told you. I wouldn't have kept that kind of information from you."

"What sets your godfather apart, Mariah," Tim told me, "is that he waits for the information to come to him. That way the timing is always perfect. He has the discipline and patience to do that. That's very rare."

"Indeed, it is," Al said, nodding to Craig. "I'll concede that."

Craig nodded in acknowledgement but no more words were spoken. We ate our donuts in silence. "Is it possible?" I asked finally. "Can I go back to the third dimension or am I stuck here?"

"Stuck?" Al said. "What makes you think you're stuck?" he asked.

"I don't know," I said in a whiny voice. "I obviously don't know what to do next so--" I stopped speaking abruptly, the breath catching in my throat. I looked at my table companions and they had all aged in the few minutes that it had taken us to eat a donut. I looked out the plate glass window. "Oh, my God!" I exclaimed. "It's dark out! It really is dark out! I can't believe it!"

"Believe it," they said in unison. We all laughed.

"Remember Mariah," Craig added. "Believing is seeing."

"How did you do that?" I asked them.

"We didn't do it," Sally said. "You did. You decided this was where you wanted to be, and so you are."

I stood up. "Thank you all," I told them, "for guiding me on this journey. I need to go home and see Rafa now."

Craig stood beside me, stuffing his laptop into his backpack. "Your whole family wants to see you Mariah," he told me. "Time appears to move more slowly in the fifth dimension. You've been missing from the third dimension a bit longer than you may realize."

I nodded, though I wasn't really getting it at that point. "Let's go," is all I said.

My three elderly friends waved goodbye and Craig and I went out the door. We walked up Broadway in the direction of my flat. "Can I ask you a couple more questions?" I asked him.

"Anything," he said.

"Well," I paused, wondering if I was brave enough to hear the answer to the question I'd yet to ask. I took a deep breath. "Craig, where is my father? Ariel was alive in the fifth dimension, but my father was still dead. Where is he?"

"Oh Mariah, that's a very big question. I really can't answer it, but I can tell you this: Ariel appeared to be alive because when she dropped her body here in this dimension she placed her consciousness in a higher dimension where she could continue her incarnation in a disease-free vehicle. But your father's energy signature has apparently let go of Charlie Easter. Or so it would appear. He may have already taken on a new incarnation, or he may be waiting on the astral planes. But it's also possible that he's still hovering around your mother, helping her and guiding her in some way."

I nodded. I could live with such speculation. "I do have one more question," I said.

"Go ahead," Craig said.

"Okay, here goes." I stopped to give him a humble smile, since I was asking a question that might be very personal. "Craig," I continued, "are you a Perfect Master?"

"Yes," he said without hesitation.

I paused, a little surprised at the unembellished directness of this response. "So, what does that mean?" I asked.

"It means that I am playing a role this incarnation. A role where I channel a lot of energy in a lot of different directions. I do this both consciously and unconsciously, and I am always increasing in awareness."

I frowned at the seeming incompleteness of this answer. "There must be more to it than that," I said insistently.

"There have been perfect masters present on earth for millennia," he said. "There have been many legends and folk tales, not to mention religious dogma, about exactly what it means to be incarnated as a perfect master. The fact is it's all about the energy. We can come up with stories to help us understand it better, but the energy is what's important."

"Okay," I said, but I felt a little disappointed.

"I know it's not enough, but that is the most accurate answer I can give you at this time," he told me. He stopped walking in front of the New Canton Cafe and looked down at me. "Mariah, now I have a question for you."

"Okay."

"Have you had your dream about the starving children again?"

I smiled. "You know it's funny you would ask. I haven't had it all month but I guess I did have a variation of it early this morning. Just before I woke up and came over to the donut shop."

"A variation?"

"Instead of a big platter of food I had this tiny slice of cinnamon toast. It smelled so good but I felt sad because I knew it wasn't enough to help even one child. So I sat down and leaned back against the door and ate the toast myself. It tasted so good, and it made me feel—I don't know—peaceful, I guess."

"Exactly!" Craig exclaimed. "Don't you see: that's the message!"

My mouth dropped open. "Wha-at?" I asked, drawing the word into two syllables in my confusion.

Craig laughed. "It's like when you're on an airplane and the flight attendant says if the oxygen masks drop down, put your own mask on first before you help anyone else."

"I see," I said. "The dream is saying, 'feed yourself first.'"

"It's an important message," Craig intoned.

I took a step back, squinting up at him under the glare of yellow street lights. "But I do feed myself! I eat healthy food and I exercise and I take care of myself. Why would my unconsciousness think I needed that message?"

"I don't know," Craig said as he started walking again. "I could only guess at that."

I had to laugh at that one. This conversation was taking on a déjà vu quality.

"Mariah," Craig continued nonchalantly, "I hear in the fifth dimension you were studying to become a Catholic priest."

"Isn't that outrageous?" I squealed. "That was the only thing that felt completely uncomfortable. I can't imagine that, can you?"

He ignored the question. "But here in the third dimension, your career options are—what are you considering?"

He turned to me, pausing again this time in front of the Taco Bell. I shrugged, still feeling non-committal. "Well, I'm thinking about teaching or social work. I'm not sure yet."

"Or maybe you'd like to be a chef or run a bakery?" he asked in a boisterous voice.

I was stunned at the suggestion. "Well, that might be fun, but--"

"But what?" he challenged.

I pressed my lips together, unsure what to say. "It's that I feel this great need to—well, I don't even know how to talk about it, Craig. I've never known how to talk about it. I want to feel useful. I want to help people. Like the starving children in my dream."

"There are many ways to help people, Mariah, but it always begins on the energetic planes. You need to follow your heart, which is another way of saying 'follow the energy.' Do what you love, Mariah! Then the answers will come."

I stared at him, so awed by this proclamation that I could think of nothing to say.

"And," he added with a sly smile, "don't forget to write it all down."

"Write it all down?" I repeated, feeling a mixture of humor and frustration at the secretive nature of this continuing request. "You know what?" I boasted. "I have been doing a lot of writing and I like it. It's been fun. But I'd still like to know why. Why do you want me to write?"

He shook his head and laughed in surrender. "Mariah," he said. "I asked you to write down what's been happening to you because I suspect you are a code writer. That means that I think you will be able to write numerological codes intuitively when you're composing creative poetry or prose. These codes will be the blue prints for the expansion of collective consciousness, and will bring great healing to those we perceive as our fellow beings. It's important work, and I know you're ready."

"But how do I do this work?" I asked.

"You just write. Don't worry about writing anything special or composing it in a special way. Just write. You will intuitively create the code. Trust your heart on this. After all, you've got some very interesting things to write down now."

"You could say that," I admitted with a laugh.

Craig stepped aside and jut his chin toward the door to the Taco Bell. "I think we'll be parting ways now," he said. I looked over and saw the man I knew as Father Ignacio just coming out of the fast food restaurant in the tattered clothes of a homeless man. "Craig," I said anxiously. "Is he really Rafa's father?"

"Follow the energy," Craig responded. "Good night, Mariah."

He headed up 26th Street, while I continued to stand in front of the neon bell, wondering how I would greet this man.

I walked slowly and tentatively. He saw me approaching, and he looked a little scared, as if I had caught him in the commission of a petty theft. He started to turn away. "Good evening, Ignacio," I called.

He turned to me startled. "You know my name, mija," he said. "How is that possible?"

"You know what," I said, suddenly letting go of my fear, "I

read your name in a church bulletin, Father."

He looked stricken. "Do you mock me, young woman?" he asked, a touch of anger in his voice.

Adrenaline burst in my throat. "Oh, no father, no, I would never mock you." I paused. "I had a dream, that's all, I had a dream that I saw your name in the church bulletin, and somehow I knew that this was the very kind man who helped me escape from that awful night club on the alley by the Capitol."

Again he looked surprised. He squinted down at me, and then gasped. "Oh si! I do remember that night, and now I recognize your face. I have been seeing you here and there for many weeks now! Our paths keep crossing. And now you know some secret about me. And you say it came to you in a dream?"

"Yes, Father."

He frowned and took a deep breath. "I am no longer called father," he said curtly. "You may call me Ignacio if you wish, but I am no one's father."

I felt in my heart the pain of this remark. "Why, Ignacio?" I asked. "Is it because you are no longer a priest or is it because you had to give up your son?"

His eyes grew wide, and he looked terrified for a moment. Then he breathed deeply again, his jaw set, and he nodded. "This is a very interesting dream you have had, young woman, but my life is not all that interesting. It's getting late; you should be going home. Good night." Again he tried to turn away, but I touched his arm.

"Ignacio, my name is Mariah, and I would be so grateful if you would tell me your story. Can I buy you dinner?"

"Gracias, Mariah," he said, "but I have eaten a taco here.

You needn't worry about me."

"Sir, I'm not worried about you!" I exclaimed. "I just want to know your story. And I want to get in out of the cold while you tell it. We can go to Los Jarritos. The food is better and the portions more generous there."

He seemed astounded by my persistence.

"Please, Ignacio, I know this sounds ridiculous, but I'm not asking for you or for myself, but rather for someone else that I love very much. I think your story may help him. Certainly you can tell your story since it may help someone else."

"You are a very strange young woman, Mariah," he told me. "I have no reason to trust you, and yet I will. I don't know why, but I will."

We walked a half block to the restaurant my own father had loved, and I insisted he order a combination plate with beans and rice and enchiladas and extra tortillas. I told him all I wanted was tortilla chips with salsa and guacamole. "Someone is making dinner for me at home," I said. Of course I had no idea if that were true in this dimension, but I hoped it was.

Ignacio proved to be a passionate and creative storyteller. He described San Dismas with great detail: bougainvillea vines draping the fence of the home where he grew up, papaya and avocado trees. He had been moved by the stories of Jesus and Francis and his love for the Eucharist to become a priest. How happy he was to serve as assistant pastor at a small church in a rural village, near avocado orchards, grape arbors, palm oil farms, and the rain forest. The people were dirt poor and the government was repressive. "We were not communists," he told me, "we only wanted assurances that the farm workers would receive a living wage, that schools be built for their children. We wanted so little."

And then he met Sonya, the biracial daughter of the

rectory's new African housekeeper. They fell in love. "I did not break my vows," he said insistently. "I asked my bishop to be released, and on his recommendation, the pope granted my request. We were married in the church, and a year later we had a son."

"And his name?" I asked. "What was the name of your son?"

"Rafael," he said, a catch in his throat. I felt myself shiver. I balled up the paper napkin I held in my hand. I forced myself to ask. "What happened to him, Ignacio? What happened to Sonya and Rafael?"

"They are both dead now, mija," he said softly as tears began to flow. "I have not told this story to anyone in nearly two decades. I'm not sure I can."

"Please, Ignacio. I must know."

"I should never have left the priesthood," he lamented. "Sonya was a pretty girl; she had any number of suitors who would have made a better husband."

"But what happened?" I insisted.

"It is because I was too arrogant. But even the bishop had confidence in me. When I left to marry, he still hired me to teach in the school, to both teach and run it. It was a small school, but we did our best, we taught the gospel, we wanted to be true to the Lord's teaching."

He was rambling now. I began to rock in my chair, as Luisa often does. I wondered what I could do to calm him, and to hasten him on to a conclusion as well. I took a deep breath and began to chant in my head.

Ignacio looked up at me. "The bishop was murdered while saying mass. This story is well known. But others were killed as well: three peasants who had been vocal against the government, a reporter for our tiny newspaper, a teacher from our school. I told Sonya we should leave. We should go stay with her cousins in the forest, just for a short while, until it all blew over. We were preparing to leave that night, under cover of darkness so they wouldn't be able to follow us. We pretended to be going about our business as usual. But that day when I came home from my work at the school, I could see from a long way off that there was blood on the door. A streak of red. I didn't allow myself to believe it could be blood at first, and yet we had seen this before. I knew this was the mark. I ran to my house and flung open the door and there lay my wife just over the threshold, her neck severed so badly, she'd been nearly decapitated. Her eyes were still staring and her mouth was open."

He was weeping openly now, speaking in a soft, but frantic voice. "What about your son?" I asked. "What about Rafa?"

He sat up abruptly to stare at me. "Rafa? Yes, that is what we called him." He swallowed hard. "His blood was everywhere. His little shirt and shoes were torn and covered in blood, but his body was gone. I don't know where they hid his body. I didn't even have a body to bury! I didn't even have the privilege of looking on his tiny face one last time! He was simply taken away from me, they both were, but at least I could bury my wife. My wife who was so young."

"Maybe Rafa is still alive," I blurted.

"No, no, I could not hope for such a blessing." He paused. "I did hope for a time of course. I searched everywhere, and I searched openly. I hoped they might kill me as well. When I couldn't find Rafa, then death became my only wish. But they would not grant it. If I'd had the courage I'd have taken my life by my own hand, but I am nothing but a coward."

"No, no," I said. "It takes much more courage to live with this much pain."

"I couldn't live with the pain, so I drank it away, mija," he confessed. "One day when I couldn't stand being there in my home village, where I could imagine my sweet wife and son at every turn, one day I started walking and I didn't stop walking until I came here to this city. Your city."

"Why here?" I asked. "I would have thought you'd choose somewhere just a little warmer."

"I don't know," he shrugged. "I have no reason anymore. I have no mind. I move here and there, as if I am an animal who is lured by a scent. And so I camped by the juncture of your rivers for ten years or more, I really don't know. And then a year or so ago, I didn't like the taste of the liquor anymore, and I stopped drinking it. I don't know why. But I moved into your city and live on the sidewalk now. I don't know why, but it suits me now. And some nights I am on the steps of your church, and some nights I am in the alley near where that nightclub used to be. I don't know why I do what I do, or go where I go. I feel moved by another hand. Perhaps God is knocking on my heart again. I don't know, but it is curious. Well, I should say that I am curious. What will happen to me now? I will wait and see."

"You are following the energy," I told him.

"Following energy?" he repeated and then he laughed. "Okay, Mariah, I suppose you could call it that." He glanced up at the clock above the salsa bar. "It is getting late. My sleeping bag is in an alley near here. I must go see if it is still a safe place to spend the night."

I took his hand. "When can I see you again?"

Ignacio squeezed my hand and then pulled his away. "I thank you for this meal, Mariah. You have been very kind. But why would you want to see me again? No, you go home to your family now."

"Ignacio, I am following the energy too!" I told him. "Promise me we can meet here again tomorrow night for dinner."

"Mariah!" he exclaimed, a bit annoyed. "No, you don't worry about me tomorrow. Tomorrow is a day for family. I will be at Loaves and Fishes. They will have a special lunch."

I felt silly later that I didn't ask why the Loaves and Fishes Services for the Homeless would have a special luncheon in the middle of the week. "I will find you again," I told him.

"It seems that we were meant to meet, Mariah." He bowed slightly and took a step back. "Be careful now, and hurry home."

I nodded. "I will," I assured him.

I took the steps two at a time, so excited to tell Rafa everything that had happened to me. The lights were on in the front room. I hoped he would be home, and even more, I hoped he would be alone.

I flung open the door and stepped inside. Rafa was slumped on the couch, his affect flat as he stared at the TV screen. Some reality show like *The Bachelor* was on. He hated shows like that. He had a half empty beer bottle in his hand. When he saw me his sleepy scowling face lit up in an expression of surprise and joy. He jumped from the couch, knocking over the beer. Within seconds he was at my side, embracing me, lifting me from the floor with his mighty arms. "Mariah, Mariah," he said in a gravelly voice, and I suddenly realized he was crying.

"What's wrong?" I asked in shock. "What's happened?"

He pulled away to look at me, though he still held me in his arms. "Where have you been?" he nearly shouted. "We'd nearly given up hope!"

"What?" I asked in confusion. "I was just down at Los

Jarritos. Before that I was with Craig. I know I was gone a little longer than I'd expected to be, but--"

"Three and a half weeks," he exclaimed. "You were gone three and a half weeks! Tomorrow is Thanksgiving!"

"Thanksgiving?" I said, sinking into a chair near the door. "But I only left this morning. I mean, that's what it felt like."

He bent down to wrap his arms around my knees. "But where were you, Mariah? Were you abducted? One of those awful men from that night club?"

"No! And how do you know about that? I didn't tell anybody--"

"I read your notebooks, your journals." I felt shocked and embarrassed. I guess it showed on my face because Rafa raised his arm as if to shield his face, seemingly afraid I might hit him. "Please don't hate me," he said, tears welling up again. "I was so scared when you disappeared. We thought something bad had to have happened. I just wanted to find you. I don't want to be without you, Mariah."

"I don't want to be without you either," I said meekly. He laid his head on my lap and I started to cry too. "You don't need to worry, Rafa. Nothing bad happened, no one abducted me. Everything is fine. It's like I fell into a wormhole or something. I had no idea that time was passing so quickly. I'm sorry; I really didn't know."

He stood up and pulled me into his arms. "All those men you talked about in your journals!" he exclaimed as he embraced me, not looking at my face. "I don't want you to see men like that."

I leaned back suddenly feeling very brave. "Well, I don't want you to keep seeing all these women either."

He smiled though he looked very surprised. "Okay."

He led me over to the couch and we sat down as close as we had in the fifth dimension when we were married. "I still don't understand where you've been," he said again. "But I have something important I've been wanting to share with you: I've started dreaming, Mariah. I started remembering my dreams!"

"Rafa!" I exclaimed. This was big. "Tell me what you dream about."

"Well, I dreamed about you," he said his voice catching again, but he breathed through it. "And then Mariah, I've been dreaming about my mother. My birth mother. I've seen my mother's face!"

"Oh, my God, Rafa! That's amazing! What did she look like?"

He leaned forward to grab a notebook from the coffee table. He opened it up and showed me a hand-drawn sketch. "This isn't very good, but she looked a little like this. I had to set it down, so I could look at her and imagine her out here someplace, and not just inside my head."

I took the paper in my hand. "She's pretty. Now tell me something, Rafa, in this sketch, it looks like she could be--"

"I know," he interrupted. "She looks like she could be part African. She looks like she could be biracial."

I held my breath. That is exactly what Ignacio had said, that Sonya was part Spanish/part African. I gripped his arm, and he tightened his hold on me. "I don't want to let you go ever again," he said and he kissed the top of my head. "But I'm being selfish. We need to call your mom and Dale. We need to let them know you're safe. But Mariah--where have you been-- a wormhole? I don't understand."

"I don't really understand either, but I'll tell you all about it later," I murmured, feeling very content to sit there with his arms wrapped around me. Now I knew I must call my family and apologize for worrying them. Rafa looked at me, then bent to touch his lips to mine. I tilted my head back to greet his kiss. There was a knock at the door, and my mother, accompanied by Craig, came rushing in. I leapt up to embrace her. She was crying with joy to see me, and I held her tight. But over her shoulder I could see Rafa smiling at me. I knew at that moment that he and I would have many years together and many stories to tell.

ACKNOWLEDGEMENTS

I am grateful that I have been befriended in this life by a Deity who has led me on a journey filled with surprising detours, creative companions, and fantastic stories I could never imagine on my own. Thank you to family, friends, high school buddies, reading and writing companions, fellow poets, philosophers, and spiritual guides. A special shout out to my surrogate sisters who go out in the street and march with me.

I love this planet and I love California. We are protected by a loving spirit. Beauty abounds. Amen.

ABOUT THE AUTHOR

Nancy Schoellkopf is a California poet and novelist who writes stories with spiritual themes. She is the author of the Avian Series of Novels--Yellow-Billed Magpie, Red-Tailed Hawk, and Ghost Owl--as well as the short story collection, Rover. In her books she has created a universe where each soul-orphaned, homeless, autistic, wounded, rich, poor, unremarkable, ageless-is discovered as a luminous gift. She invites the reader to ponder the extraordinary treasures hidden in the ordinary events of daily life.

Based in Sacramento, Nancy spent over 30 years teaching amazing children in Special Education Classes in urban school districts. A full-time writer now, she enjoys lavishing attention on her cats, her garden, and her intriguing circle of family and friends.

Contact her at her website: www.nancyschoellkopf.com